Silver Jubilee

Twenty-Five Years of Stories

Paul Magrs

Contents

Imaginary Boys

The Middle of Nowhere

Catskin

TV Writer

All the Lady Writers of the Grange-Over-Sands Hotel Workshop

Companion Piece

Sit Down Next to Me

The Girl in the Pink Coat

The Wizard of Arncliffe Place

Understanding

Thistle Street, 1995

Imaginary Boys

David Taylor was walking home from sixth form college, through drifts of orange leaves during the season known as autumn. He was seventeen, of medium height and build, with brown hair that needed cutting. His eyes were downcast and dark as stewed tea. He wore a blurred, vague sort of expression as if his thoughts were far away.

It was starting to get dark and David kept looking over his shoulder as he hurried back to the council estate where he lived with his female parent.

This seemed like the most stressful week of David's life. Besides everything going on at home with his mam, there was Lawrence as well. The new boy in the Sixth Form. Awkward and hanging onto the sidelines and always there. David had felt watched by him these past two weeks. Was he imagining it?

'Why are you walking along with me, Lawrence? I never asked you to.'

David stopped walking and Lawrence almost bumped into him.

'And will you stop… narrating me?' snapped David. 'It's driving me mad.'

I'm sorry about that, David.

'Are you trying to wind me up?'

I can assure you I am not. It's a compliment, really.

'To have you following me around?'

Lawrence could see that David was at the end of his tether.

'Just get lost, will you? Leave me alone.'

But this is where I'm meant to be.

'You what?'

I'm doing my job. And it's all to do with you, David.

'I mean it – shut up. *And go away*!'

There was a slight pause.

I'm sorry if I seem like a 'weirdo' to you, David. That is what you think, isn't it?

'I don't think you're a weirdo.'

I'm Lawrence. I'm new in town.

'I know, you're in my class. Where are you from?'

Verbatim 6.

'What?'

It's a small planet about three-hundred light years from here. I'm your Novelizor, David.

David looked unconvinced. 'Okay.' He frowned. 'Bye, then!'

David turned and walked quickly away.

*

His mam was watching a quiz show when David came home.

'Where have you been?' she called from the front room. 'Your tea's all black in the oven.'

He shrugged. 'I'm not really hungry.'

'Here. Have one of these. I've left you all the soft centres.'

He peered at he mostly-empty box of chocolates. 'Have you finished another box?'

'I can't help it.'

'I'll get you some more when I'm in town.'

'Are you all right? I usually get a lecture about how my cravings are no good for me.'

'I'm fine, Mam, really.'

'No one's been picking on you or anything, have they? Or giving you any trouble?'

'No, no. Nothing like that. Just some strange lad on the way home. New guy in our year…'

'Cause if those rough lads are bothering you again I'll…'

'Mum, I'm seventeen. I can look after myself.'

She watched him carefully as he went to leave the room.
'Where are you off to now?'

'Up to my room.'

'Yeah, don't whatever you do spend any time with your poor old pregnant mother who's been sat here alone all day.'

Lawrence was watching this unfold from outside. He was crouching down by the window, in some bushes. He hadn't been invited in yet. He wasn't close enough to his subject. Not as close as a Novelizor needs to be.

Through the window he could see a room with a large television screen and sliding panels of glass that opened onto a flat concrete area with green moss growing on it and plastic chairs. He saw the distended form of the female parent supine upon a settee that was decorated with a floral design. She was fabricating a tiny pair of shoes out of strings of coloured twine using two metal rods that made an insistent ticking noise. Then she left the room and walked upstairs.

She knocked on her son's bedroom door.

'Can I come in?'

'No,' he said.

She opened the door.

'What are you doing?'

He was on his bed. There was a bunch of old books from the library on his duvet, as usual. 'Reading poetry,' he said, holding one up. 'Keats. Ode to Autumn. 'Season of mists and mellow fruitfulness."

'Oh yes?' she laughed at his put-on poetry voice.

He went on: 'Close-bosom friend of the maturing sun...'

'Sounds a bit saucy. Bosoms in poetry.'

'Mam..!'

'You and your poetry,' she said, rolling her eyes. She wanted to sit down with him. Ruffle his already-messy hair. 'You've had to be the man of the house since your dad went. But you have to be even more so now, with the baby nearly here.'

'I know that, Mam.'

'It's a long time since I went through the agony of giving birth to you and it's scary just the thought of going through it again.'

'I'm here, Mam.'

'There's all the bringing up baby, too. I'm going to be what they call an older mother.'

'We'll manage.'

'I suppose you'll be swanning off to university soon and I won't see you any more...'

He burst out: 'Oh, give it a rest!' Then he took a deep breath. 'Sorry, Mam. I'll be home to visit.'

'I was used to being a young mother. With you I was sixteen and I got all the catty remarks. I had to fight everyone to keep you.'

'I know, Mam.'

'It's always been me and you, David.'

'You and me against the world.'

'Your Dad never really fit in, even when he was here. He was always so bound up in his bloody police work. We hardly even noticed him gone last Christmas, did we?'

'Cos we still had each other.'

'Oh, come here. Give your old Mam a hug…' Just then a funny look went across her face. 'Oh…!'

He sat up quickly. He was on his feet. 'What is it?'

'I think… I think it's coming… the baby's coming!'

'Are you sure?'

She looked stricken. She was grabbing hold of the bedroom door. 'David, call an ambulance!'

'You know what happened last time.'

She was holding onto the door, shaking her head. 'Ow! This is really it. Owww!'

'You're sure this isn't another of your false alarms?'

'Call it,' she shouted. 'Call them up, David, now!'

*

For the third night that month, David and his Mum raced to the hospital prematurely. Another late night while the doctors looked at her and felt her all over and told her the baby wasn't ready yet, and she should get herself home. Another ride back home in a taxi.

Next day, in the Sixth Form common room, David seemed to be prone to opening his mouth and making sudden, wordless noises and then looking embarrassed. This, Lawrence discovered was 'yawning.'

Then David went off to somewhere called the 'Boys' Bogs' and Lawrence followed him for a quiet word.

He stood outside the cubicle David was in and gave a polite knock.

David?

'What?'

It's Lawrence.

'Can't I get some peace?'

I wanted to explain something.

David flushed the toilet and came out of the little room, banging the door.

'Yeah?' he snapped. 'You can explain why you're following me about for a start.'

It's my job, David. This is what I'm here on Earth to do.

'Yeah, yeah…'

I've come a very long way to see you David. To watch your early years here. It's all very interesting.

'Did anyone see you follow me in here?'

The thing is, David, I'm only in *disguise* as a new pupil. This isn't who I really am at all. My job is to collect stories and keep a record of interesting lives. And, well, I chose you.

There was a long pause.

Then David asked, 'You chose me?' He frowned and stared at Lawrence. 'What for?'

Said David, his heart rate increasing and his pulse pounding in his ears.

'And why do you keep on doing that?!'

Narrating, you mean? I have to keep an account of your actions.

'I really don't need this right now. Just stay out of my way, okay?'

He started to leave the 'Boys' Bogs.'

Aren't you going to wash your hands first? I believe that is the custom.

*

The following morning at breakfast, David's mam was fixating on the idea that her son might put another person – an undetermined female person – in a condition she described several times as 'the pudding club.'

'Mam, seriously, I'm running late. Can't this wait till later?'

'All I'm saying is, you're seventeen now, and I don't want you getting caught out like I did.'

'Yeah, well. I won't.'

'You don't know what girls are like.'

'You're right about that.'

'I'm just saying. You've got to watch out. Don't chuck your life away like I did.'

'Thanks!'

'You know what I mean.'

'Mam, I'm going to get caught out, as you put it. When would I ever get the chance, even if I wanted to?'

'Don't get smart,' she snapped.

Their late-night false alarms and ambulance trips ensured they were both over-tired and cross almost every morning.

Then the front door went.

'Who's that knocking at breakfast time?'

'I'll go,' David said.

It was me! Lawrence the Novelizor from Verbatim 6. I had decided to take things to the next level in my campaign to get closer to my subject, and had learned of these things called 'friends'. I had decided that I would become David's, and to that end, I had brought a small offering.

'Lawrence! What are you doing here?'

I want to become closer to you, David.

Mam was shouting from the kitchen. 'Who is it? It's not religious, is it?'

I've brought you an offering, David.

'Oh! I don't really want... '

Here!

'What is it?'

It's a journal. You have to write in it.

'Okay...'

You've always wanted to be a writer, haven't you? These empty pages are for you to fill with all your secrets and dreams and ideas.

'Right,' said David. 'Thanks.'

David looked – as he would put it – 'freaked out' by the whole thing.

'Do I look freaked out?' he asked.

Of course. But you're getting used to me, I think. Can I walk to college with you?

'Go on then. Hang on. I'll get my bag.' He yelled back at the kitchen: 'I'm off now, Mam!'

She yelled back: 'Aren't you going to kiss me goodbye?'

'See you tonight!'

The boys walked in silence for a while across a building site and then Lawrence said that he thought David should have introduced him to his 'Mam'.

'I don't think so,' said David.

But I need to know everything about you. She gave you life, didn't she? She was one of your progenitors.

'That's why I can't introduce you to her, Lawrence. You'll go saying something like that.'

I think I'm getting the hang of life on earth.

David pulled a face. 'I wish I was.'

David and Lawrence climbed through a broken fence and across damp playing fields to get to the low, blocky buildings of the school. As they joined crowds of younger human beings, Lawrence sensed David draw away from everyone else. He really seemed happiest when he was being most distant. In his classes he sat on his own. Which was good, because this made space for his

Novelizor to pull up a seat alongside him. He did this in every classroom David went to and, eventually, David seemed all right with that.

    Do you mind if I sit here?

    'Fine. As long as you don't describe everything I do.'

    Said David.

    Sorry. Couldn't resist.

*

David had another friend, called Robert, who was into 'bands' and was very keen on football as well. At the end of that particular day at college David was walking alongside Robert, and Lawrence lagged along behind, listening in.

    Robert was describing something he had seen happening during a game of football. Apparently somebody involved had 'nutmegged the defender' and 'planted it in the top corner.'

    David appeared to follow the meaning of this about as much as Lawrence did. 'Wow! Great. Er, is that good?'

    But then Robert had noticed who was following them down the street. 'Don't look now, Davey boy. But your mate's following you again!'

'Oh,' said David. 'Yeah.'

'Do you want me to have a word?' Robert asked him. 'Or something a little harder?'

Lawrence gathered that by this Robert was offering to do something violent. David was alarmed. 'No, it's okay. He's all right.' He stopped and turned round. 'Lawrence? You can walk with us if you like.'

Pleased, Lawrence hurried to catch up with them.

'What are you doing?' said Robert.

'He's all right. Give him a chance.'

Here we all are then! Walking home through the dark streets of the estates and the deep autumn leaves and talking about... what are we talking about?

'Football,' said a glum-looking David.

'And I was telling David he should come and watch the match down the Turbinia,' said Robert.

Should he?

'I can't,' said David. 'I should be getting home for Mam.'

Robert was keen for his friend to come to the pub and see the game. 'Come on. You should come down, we'll get leathered.'

What is 'leathered'?

David told Lawrence: 'He means drunk.'

But David is only seventeen. It would be against human law for him to consume alcoholic beverages.

Robert looked at the Novelizor incredulously. 'Just... forget it.'

Lawrence turned his attention to his subject. I can't help noticing that you're dawdling, David. Won't your 'mam' be worrying?

Robert looked from one to the other. 'What is it with you two? It's like he's got some sort of hold over you, Davey.'

Lawrence nodded eagerly and happily explained how, in the old days, Novelizors used to have a literal hold over their subjects and if anyone tried to escape their brains would be burned out. Very nasty. Of course, it wasn't like that nowadays.

Robert tried to pull David aside. 'What the hell's he on about?'

Embarrassed, David said: 'Just some science fiction thing. Lawrence is into sci-fi.'

'Oh, he's a geek as well, is he? Fine. I'll leave you to your boyfriend.'

'Shut up,' David said, looking cross.

Lawrence shrugged. I am indeed a boy, and I'm his friend. What of it?

Robert was bored with the pair of them by now. There was something funny about the way they were going on and he didn't like it. 'Look, I've got better stuff to do. See you tomorrow, maybe.'

'Robert, wait...!' David called, but it was hopeless because Robert was already running off and turning the corner at the end of the street.

David was left walking along with Lawrence, who grinned at him.

Robert seems nice. What would you like to talk about? Shall we continue that very interesting conversation from our English class? About Woolf and the Brontes and how every human relationship seems, in your opinion, to be ultimately doomed to failure?

'No,' snapped David. 'It's fine. I'll see you later, maybe. I ought to be getting home...'

*

'Hey, buggerlugs,' Mam said. On the telly someone was taking something out of an oven really carefully while a couple of other people watched on. 'Come and watch the Cakey-Bakey show with me.'

'No thanks.'

'What's the matter with you?'

'Oh, I'm just knackered, that's all. Too much coursework and... stuff.'

'Stuff?' Mam pressed the mute button on the remote. 'I thought as much. Is it... a girl?'

'No!'

'Huh – I know troubles in love when I see them. Oh come on, David, you can confide in your mam!' She reached for her box of Celebrations.

'It's nothing. It's just...'

'What?'

'Dad was... he was your first, wasn't he?'

She laughed bitterly, fishing around in the chocolates. 'Yeah first and only – and look how that went!' She stared at him. He looked so awkward standing there. 'Hey, you're not worrying about ending up like him, are you? You're more like me than him. You've got my nicer nature.'

'Yeah, so I've heard.' He rolled his eyes. She'd been saying that stuff forever. 'So... if you could go back in time, would you... would you change things?'

'Of course not! It was worth going through every moment of those eighteen years with that stupid tosser. Because out of all of that I got you, didn't I?'

David smiled. 'Thanks, Mam.'

'Think nothing of it. My best years were wasted, my confidence was ruined and my looks have gone to pot, but you make it all worthwhile, son.' She gave him a great big smile and then she turned the sound back on, just in time for judges' comments.

*

It was a few days later that David next saw Lawrence at college. The Novelizor had been minding his own business, observing David's world. David found him sitting alone in the common room.

Lawrence thought he would sit here quietly, trying to blend in.

'I want to ask you something...' David said.

Have you started writing in your journal yet?

'Listen, I've got a free afternoon so I came to ask you if – you wanted to...'

It's important that you start writing quite soon. You've got a lot of work ahead of you, you know.

'I've an afternoon off. And actually, I was going to ask you...'

Yes? What were you going to ask me?

'If you wanted to come to Darlington on the bus with me. There's a place I'd like to show you.'

Lawrence could hardly believe it.

I would be delighted, David.

'Really?' David grinned. 'Great!'

*

David and Lawrence caught the 723 bus to Darlington. In the marketplace they visited a small shop. David led the way inside, as if it was a place of worship. There were pale wooden shelves and a long table in the middle, with paperbacks laid out in luridly colourful rows. The air was scented with exotic spices and that was apparently because these were foreign imports. These books had travelled from far afield.

David said, 'I brought you here because you like sci-fi.'

Do I?

'This bookshop is the best. They're all American remainder copies. And comics, too.' He started poring over the stacks, and picking up particular books that caught his attention. 'Have you read this? 'The Grisly Space Fandango' by Penelope Faith Conquest? Or this series, 'The Eternal Mayhem Chronicles' by Everard Donat.' He stopped and looked around at the close confines of the shop around him. 'I've been coming here for years...'

Lawrence studied everything that David pointed out to him.

Some of these illustrated covers are very interesting, David. The being on this one who is strangling the Earth astronaut has a look of my fifth eldest aunt on my female parent's side.

'What?!'

That was me joking. She has far too few secondary sexual characteristics.

'Right... ... Oh, look: 'Entrails by Moonlight.' By Marcia Sopwith.'

Lawrence peered over his shoulder.

I like finding out what you like.

David was pleased to hear this. He'd never had anyone share his enthusiasm for books like this before. 'Come and take a look at the Paranormal Romance section! Some of these are brilliant!'

Lawrence frowned.

What is... Paranormal Romance?

'It's where people fall in love with unsuitable beings,' David explained. 'Vampires, werewolves, shape-shifters and stuff. And it usually all goes wrong.'

I myself am a shape-shifter. Have I told you that?

'Er... no.'

I can turn into just about anything.

*

Later, in the café next door, David and Lawrence had organic cheese scones and Lady Grey tea and David talked once more about the futility of human love.

David started quoting: "I am the only being whose doom / No tongue would ask, no eye would mourn..."

Lawrence stirred his tea.

Pardon? Could I have the sugar, please?

'Emily Bronte,' said David.

Ah, yes. A very nice lady. I did some of my early fieldwork in nineteenth century Yorkshire, probing into the psyches of the Bronte sisters.

'Right...' David said. He supposed he was getting used to Lawrence's strange sense of humour. 'I guess she was saying that we're, like, all on our own in the end.'

Novelizors can't stand being on their own. Lawrence frowned and examined his scone. We begin to lose our faculties if we have no one to observe.

'I actually think human beings are made to be on their own,' said David. 'We're better off being solitary. Everyone ends up falling apart otherwise. Look at Mam and Dad. And Mam and my Nanna. It all goes wrong. Even Mam and me are falling out more lately.'

Not good examples there, David, since the common denominator is your mam. Might it just be that she causes rows with everyone?

'She's had a tough time!'

David was cross whenever Lawrence criticized his mother.

'I'm all she's got since Dad walked out, just after she told him about the baby. And she had me so young. I owe her so much. She was like sixteen and her own mother chucked her out and wouldn't even visit the hospital...'

Is this why you read such sad poetry all the time? Because of your guilt and attachment to your mother? Perhaps you are identifying too heavily with her view of the universe?

'I... er... don't know about that...'

I haven't been on planet Earth for very long, but I will venture an opinion. I don't think quite all human relationships are doomed.

'I feel like mine are,' sighed David. 'It's like I've grown up wrong, somehow.'

Lawrence was surprised to hear that. He thought David was probably okay, actually.

David looked up at him, surprised to hear this. 'Erm, thanks.'

They stopped to look at each other over the table. Lawrence suddenly thought that David's eyes really did look like the very dark, very sweet tea he favoured.

David took a deep breath. 'You know... I think I might fancy you. A bit. Is that okay?'

Lawrence wasn't sure how to react to that.

'I've never said anything like that to anyone before.'

This was obviously a big moment in David's emotional development. It was most interesting.

'Right,' said David briskly. 'Well, let's just forget it, shall we? I never said anything.'

Lawrence made a note of it.

'Just forget it...!' snapped David.

*

That night David started writing in the journal Lawrence had given him.

'I kept a Page-a-Day diary when I was a kid, years ago. I stopped because I thought nothing was happening in my life. It was all about what was on TV and having pizza for tea and Mam fighting with Dad and everything they said.

'Maybe now is when things start to happen. I feel jumpy and tingly, like my whole body knows something. Does that sound daft? Maybe I should write this in cipher. I know Mam goes through my stuff when she's bored. And if you're reading this, Mam, don't try to deny it...

'I met this boy called Lawrence. He says he comes from a world called Verbatim 6. He says that he has chosen me.'

*

The following evening Lawrence was following David home as usual, looking forward to another of their chats.

'Oi!'

But then he saw David get stopped by an older boy called Simon Grainger – and his spotty mate, whose name David never knew.

They were bored and dizzy after an afternoon spent drinking a local beverage known as White Lightning.

'Hey, it's that posh get. You. Yes, you.'

David tried to move past them. But they planted themselves either side of him.

'Excuse me.'

'Listen to his manners. He sounds like a puff.'

The spotty friend laughed at this. Lawrence stood watching from the top of the hill as Simon shoved David and he fell down in the mud.

'Whoops – look out. You've slipped on the leaves!'

David tried to tell him to leave him alone.

'Come on then, you faggot. Fight back, won't you?'

David couldn't get up.

'Where's your boyfriend today, then?'

'He's just a mate, that's all.'

Lawrence realized they were talking about him.

'You ought to watch out. We don't have queers round here.'

'Get off me!'

David stayed on the ground. They kicked him. And they spat on him. All the shouted words were blending into one then. Faggot. Puff. Queer.

They kept kicking him.

The bigger boy was shouting, 'Come on! Get up!'

The other one noticed that kids were gathering round and taking pictures of the fight on their telephones and posting them on social networking sites and getting 'likes'.

The Novelizor watched all of this from the top of the hill. He was making careful mental notes. He wondered if David was getting hurt.

This had to happen. He knew that it did. It was a part of the story.

There was such a lot going on. A small crowd had gathered. Some girl was calling the police on her phone.

And then the two aggressors both turned and ran away.

Lawrence came to join his subject. His face was bleeding.

I saw what happened. Are you all right?

Lawrence tried to help David up but he was shrugged off angrily. Kids were still staring, fascinated. Then the last of them ran off.

'Why didn't you do something?'

Did they really attack you because you are a queer puff?

'It's because you hang around me, making them think you're my bloody boyfriend. It's all your fault and when I could do with some help you're not even there...!'

I am a Novelizor. I can't get involved. I can only watch and narrate.

David looked at him in disbelief. 'You what? Oh, just piss off, Lawrence. Leave me alone.'

David picked himself up and limped home. He was winded from having his balls kicked. And I – Lawrence the Novelizor - followed him home. Always a few steps behind.

'Piss the hell off, Lawrence.'

*

Lawrence wanted to see that David was safely home. His mam was so shocked by the state of him she almost went into labour there and then. But she didn't. She did something even more disturbing.

She went and phoned David's dad, who David hadn't seen since he moved out the previous year.

'I know you don't want to see him – neither do I! He made both our lives a misery.'

'Then why did you phone him?' He was horrified at the idea of his dad turning up.

'He's a copper. He's got power. He can get them – those animals – who did this to you.'

'I'm all right. Phone him again and say we don't need him.'

'You're not all right. Look at you.'

'Just cuts and bruises.'

'You were lucky to get away. And where was that friend of yours? That so-called best pal?'

'Lawrence?' David shrugged. 'Lawrence didn't want to fight, he...'

'Some pal he turned out to be.'

'It wasn't his fault.'

There came an abrupt knocking from the front door.

Mam squeaked. 'That'll be your Dad. I've got to get changed. Answer it, will you?'

'Why are you getting changed?'

'I want to show him what he's missing.'

'What?!'

She was halfway up the stairs. 'Just answer the door.'

David took a deep breath before opening the front door. And there was Dad. In his work suit. Looking more or less the same as ever.

'David. God, look at you. What the hell happened?'

'I've been beaten up.'

His dad gave a mirthless laugh. 'I can see that!' He stepped forward. 'Can I come in?'

'I guess.'

Dad led the way to their front room. 'When your Mam phoned the station she was lucky to get me. I should be literally in

Sunderland right now.' He turned to study David's face. 'That's a nasty shiner you're going to have there, son.'

David looked away from him. 'There's not much to make a statement about...'

'Young thugs can't go round attacking people like that. I understand that's what happened.' He sat down heavily on the armchair and tugged his trousers neat. Then he fetched a little notebook and pen out of his jacket.

'It was unprovoked,' David told him. 'They got me on the way home from school.'

'Did they say anything?'

'Nothing. Just laid into me.'

'And do you know who they are?'

'Simon Grainger and some mate of his. They left school last year.'

'I see,' said Dad. 'There was a lad hanging about outside the house when I pulled up.'

'What?'

'Blond lad.'

'Oh. That's just Lawrence. He wasn't involved.'

'Ok,' said Dad, as David came back from peering through the net curtains. 'Now, you are going to tell me the details slowly and I'll write them down and then yourself can sign it and we'll see about getting these lads picked up tonight, all right? I'll get them. They can't do this to you. Not to my son.'

'They already have.'

'This wouldn't have happened if I was still here. I could…'

'It would have happened anyway.'

His dad looked cross with him. 'I could have taught you better how to stick up for yourself. I should have…'

Mam came breezing in, wearing a floaty, aqua print maternity dress. She looked glamorous with her hair down. She gave off a kind of carefree vibe.

'Oh!' she said, looking at them both in the middle of their interview. 'There you are…'

Dad nodded at her. 'Mary.'

'Have you seen what those scumbags have done to your son?'

'We'll sort it out.' He looked her up and down briefly. 'You look nice, Mary.'

Her eyebrows shot up. 'Me? I'm in my rags. And I'm huge. The important thing here is David. Your son. Have you forgotten about him, eh? Look at him. You've not seen him since before Christmas. Not so much as a card!'

'Look, Mary, I've got to get this statement done and then…'

'Oh, you get on and do what you have to. I remember all your bloody 'procedures' and paperwork. Nothing ever changes with you, does it?

I suppose you'll be wanting a cup of tea.'

'Milky. Lots of sugar. For the shock.'

Mam laughed. '*He's* the one who's had the shock!'

'I *meant* him,' said Dad.

Mam waltzed off to make tea.

So David made his statement to his Dad, who laboured over it, scribbling away. David was dismayed to see his words being changed, simplified, mispelled. His Mam brought the tea and went on sitting there in her colourful frock the whole time with the best china out, and French Fancies on a plate. The telly sound was down and she was shooting glances at his dad.

When the statement was all taken, Dad stood up again and studied Mam. 'And you, Mary. You must be… close to time now.'

'Yes.'

'You'll let me know, won't you. When the baby comes…'

'Will do.'

'I could be there…'

'I'll let you know. If you're that interested. Look, if you've finished taking his statement just go, would you?'

Lawrence the Novelizor had been waiting outside. He waited until the policeman left and drove off.

'Er, hullo. Is David home?'

Mam wasn't impressed by Lawrence standing there on the doorstep. 'Oh, so this is your mate who didn't help you, is it?'

David let him in. 'Mam, it's fine. Come on, Lawrence. We'll go to my room.'

*

David flomped down on his single bed and let out a huge sigh. He lay on top of scribbled essay notes, paperbacks and his new journal.

'That was awful.'

Lawrence had never been in David's bedroom before. It was messy and dark and musky-smelling.

'Just shut up, will you, Lawrence?'

Lawrence sat down carefully on the desk chair.

I was interested to see your male parent. Will you look like that when you are older? Balding and blotchy?

'I don't even know why I'm still talking to you.'

I believe it's because you don't have many other friends in your peer group. Tell me more about your reunion with your male parent. This is a very significant moment.

'He wanted to know what names they were shouting at me. Not how I was getting on at college, or how Mam and I are doing without him. Just what words they chose to use when they beat the crap out of me. And what was I going to say? Puff? Queer?'

Did you?

'What do you think?'

Lawrence thought about this. He thought about everything that had been happening during the past few, interesting hours.

He seemed like a nice man, your father.

'No he didn't. And then he said – he said…'

What?

'He said I needed a proper man's influence in my life. That I'd been missing having him around all year and that was doing me harm.'

Is that true? Do you miss him?

'I don't know. Not really. But… I end up actually feeling guilty. Because I haven't been in touch with him either, have I? I agreed to go out on Saturday with him. To the shops.'

You are going to spend 'quality' time with your male parent.

'He's offered to help me choose a suit for my university interviews.'

You don't look very pleased about this.

'I just want to die.'

I'll come with you, if you like.

'When I die?'

I meant in the car with your dad. To the shops. On Saturday.

'No! Absolutely no way. No!'

*

Lawrence looked out of the car window at the motorway, streaking by.

I've never been in a police car before.

'It's not a police car. It's a Mondeo,' said David's dad, keeping his eye on the road. Next to him, David was being very quiet. 'What do you think of this suit I'm wearing, David?'

'Very smart, yeah.'

'I thought we'd get something like it for yourself.'

'Great'.

Lawrence had noticed that David's dad would use the word 'yourself' instead of 'you'. It sounded strangely formal and oblique, as in: 'I'm taking yourself to the biggest shopping mall in Europe!' and 'Can yourself drive a car yet?'

'What's your friend saying back there?' Dad frowned.

'He often talks to himself, don't you, Lawrence?'

'I don't mind bringing him along, even though it's literally the only time we've had together in months.'

'Thanks,' said David.

'Do you see much of that Robert Woolf still? He was a good lad. Still into his football is he? He had a natural talent, I always thought.'

'We've kind of drifted,' said David. 'He hangs around with a dodgy crowd.'

'That's not good.'

'Yeah.'

'Your mother's looking well. I hope you'll both cope. Just the two of you.'

'We can manage.'

Dad shot a glance at him. 'Not fair on a young lad like yourself, though, is it?'

'It's okay.'

'I would have stayed, you know. For the little one. And for you, as well. It's just…'

'What? It's just what, Dad?'

'It would have been worse if I'd stayed. You know that. Me and your mam, you know, it just couldn't go on like that…'

David wasn't sure what he was supposed to say to all of this. 'Well, it's better now.'

'That's how you feel, is it?'

'But it is, isn't it? Your life is better too. Away from Mam.'

'Yes… you'll be away soon as well, won't you? Which universities are you applying to?'

'Lancaster, York, Middlesbrough…'

'You'll look the part in your new suit. I could drive you there, to the interviews and stuff.'

'Yeah?'

'What are dads for?'

David bit his tongue.

*

At the shopping mall Dad made him try suits on and David was mortified by styles, prices, by the things his dad said. By the matey way he had of going on.

'What you want is something that will last for years. Quality, not something trendy…'

'I suppose.'

Dad's favourite menswear shops weren't appealing to David very much.

'You needn't spend a fortune to look stylish and smart. Are you listening, son?'

But David had seen someone.

'Oh no.'

'Isn't that your mate? Robert? Go and talk to him, David. He's waving you over.'

Robert Woolf was hanging around with some girls, next to a fountain.

'Davey,' Robert greeted him.

'You remember my dad?'

Robert nodded. 'Mr Taylor.'

'Hello there, Robert. What are you up to then? Shouldn't you be at football practice? I remember yourself being a smashing centre forward at one time. Do you still play?'

'A bit. When I can.'

'We're getting David kitted out with some new gear.'

Robert grinned. 'Gear, eh? And what about his pal? Are you kitting him out as well?'

The two girls giggled, and everyone turned to look at the Novelizor.

'That's Lawrence,' Dad said. 'He's David's new friend.'

'Yeah, I know,' Robert said. There was something funny about his tone of voice. 'His 'friend.''

David was turning away. 'Look, can we just go now?'

Dad chuckled. 'He's just in a bad mood.'

Robert called out: 'You could hang out with us if you want, Davey.'

Lawrence piped up.

David is going to the Terrace Café for High Tea with his father and his friend, Lawrence. That's what's going to happen now.

'Uh... right,' said Robert. 'Go on then. Do what you want.'

David, Dad and Lawrence moved away from the small party by the fountain, in the direction of the Food Court.

'You should be nicer to him,' Dad said. 'He's just a pleasant, normal lad.'

David didn't look convinced.

Dad snapped, 'Would you stop butting in all the time, son?'

'Leave him alone!' David said, louder than he'd meant to.

Dad was getting angry now. 'I'll tell you what you've got to learn to do better, David. And that's mixing in more. There's all types of people in this world. Don't be getting ideas about yourself.'

David had had enough for one day. 'Can we... can we just go home now?'

*

So they didn't choose a suit in the end. They went home empty-handed. All the way home Dad talked about his police work.

'When you're in a position like mine, you've got to be sure about things. I banged up a vicious cross-dresser from Ferryhill who was abusing his foster kiddies. There's no shades of grey in a case like that. It's stark black and white. He's the baddy and I'm literally the goody.'

He was playing them his 'Simply Red' CD.

Are we nearly home yet?

'I think Lawrence is feeling car-sick,' said David.

'We're almost back,' Dad told him. He didn't really care if Lawrence felt unwell or not. 'Look, did they really call yourself a puff?'

'Who?'

'Your assailants. They admitted in their own statements that they used terms of homophobic abuse and all that.' There was a pause then, and David stared at the green fields sliding by, and clouds that looked to him like galleons. 'Look, son. You can tell your dad anything. If yourself has anything to say…'

'I've got nothing to say.'

It was like a police interrogation.

'I'm just asking.'

'Well. Okay,' said David.

'Cos if yourself has any worries on that score – they are wrong. Those lads. You're just sensitive and clever, like your mam used to be. That doesn't make yourself a homosexual or anything. You needn't worry. You can still be a normal lad.'

'You what?!'

'I don't think you've grown up wrong and perverted. I really don't.' Now they were pulling into their town. They were almost home.

'Oh. Okay. Thanks,' said David. Then, a few minutes later, they were parked outside David and his mam's house. 'Bye, Dad.'

'Bye then, son.'

The car raced off again.

Lawrence thought he preferred David's female parent.

'You're not the only one,' David told him.

That night was the night David's female parent went into the throes of the state known as labour – and this time it was real.

'What?!' David gasped.

*

They could hear Mam screaming in the front room, even before David got the front door open. The pair of them went running through. She was on the settee and the cushions had been flung all over. Her knitting and all the remotes were on the floor.

'Mam! What's happening?'

'What do you bloody well think is happening?!'

Lawrence the Novelizor had been quite correct in his earlier assessment of the situation.

'Lawrence, just stop! Mam..?!'

Mam was gasping with pain. 'You've been too busy running about with that pig of a father of yours.'

'Oh god,' said David. He was frozen in the doorway.

'Can you - phone an - ambulance...' Mam panted. 'I couldn't find the cordless nnnnnggh bloody thing – or my – flipping mobile...'

'Will an ambulance get here in time? Mam!'

David's mother was hauling herself onto the settee with her legs up. Her 'waters' had apparently broken and her knitting was ruined.

Mam was struggling to sit up. 'Your father spoiled - nnngg - both our lives. Aaagghh. I hate bloody men. Don't just stand there, David!'

For a few moments he couldn't move. He couldn't even think straight.

'David, man! It's going to happen right now. What did he say about me? Nnnng. Your so-called father? Aaaagghh. Slagging me off, I suppose?'

'What do I do?'

She was trying to get both her legs onto the settee, grunting and breathing hard. 'Did he buy you anything? NNNGG.'

'Shut up about Dad. He doesn't matter.'

'He's useless. AAGGGHHH.'

David seemed to come back to his senses. 'Hot water and clean towels. That's what we need.'

Lawrence wasn't sure what you did with the hot water and towels once you actually had them. Neither was David.

'Mam, can you wait until the ambulance comes?'

'AAAAGGGHHHH!'

'And shouldn't you be doing your special breathing or something?'

'NNNNGGG! What special bloody breathing?'

It was getting very noisy in their sitting room by now.

Mam had both hands on her huge belly. 'This won't wait for the ambulance.'

David was worried in case it was like the boy who cried wolf and the paramedics had stopped believing her.

'Lawrence, shut up!' David shouted at his friend. 'Stop saying stupid stuff and help me! Boil the kettle and I'll phone.'

Lawrence stared at him, trying to be calm.

I shouldn't interfere. I'm not supposed to.

'Just do it! You have to help! You can't just stand there!'

Lawrence just stood there, feeling unhappy and torn.

You don't understand, David!

'I do. You're scared. I'm scared. But you have to help.'

But Novelizors aren't supposed to get involved! You saw me! I just stood there, didn't I? When they hit you and kicked you?

'It doesn't matter about that now,' David told him.

Lawrence stared at the carpet and the sopping bundle of knitting.

I tried so hard not to get involved.

Then Mam started shrieking: 'HURRY UP! NNNGG!'

'It's really true, isn't it?' said David, in an awe-struck tone of voice. 'It's really going to happen. On our settee.'

Lawrence nodded.

She is going to give birth to another person, yes. A smaller one.

David was at the sideboard, fumbling with the cordless phone.

'Maybe it'll take ages,' he said. 'They sometimes do, don't they? Maybe the ambulance will have time to get here…'

Mam was screaming at the top of her lungs by now.

Lawrence shuddered.

It could put you off for life, this.

Mam's screams ebbed away for a few moments and she caught her breath. Her face was bright red and wet with perspiration. 'I wish I'd bothered with more of them classes now. I thought I'd remember everything from last time.'

'That was seventeen years ago,' David told her. 'Do your breathing!'

'You popped out easy as anything,' she told him.

'Mam! You have to remember! Your breathing! Do it… !'

'I can't!'

'Mam – look – I don't know what to do, I…'

'Nnnnggggg! Aaaaaaaah!'

David turned to his friend for help. 'Lawrence… I … I can't… What do I do?!'

Lawrence the Novelizor from Verbatim 6 took a huge breath and made the biggest decision of his life.

Stand back, David.

'What are you doing?'

I'm taking off my school tie. And I'm rolling up the sleeves of my shirt.

'But what are you going to do..?' David shouted.

I'm getting involved.

Mam yelled out croakily: 'I'm going to die.'

No, you're not.

She had her hair plastered all over her face and gently, Lawrence helped her brush it aside.

Can you push?

I don't know. I'll have to take my pants off.'

'Oh god,' David said.

Mam screamed and David stepped backwards, watching in horrified fascination as Lawrence took over looking after his mam.

'Listen,' Mam grunted. 'Listen – if I die…'

You're not going to die.

'Women die in childbirth all the time,' she pointed out, her voice full of panic.

Lawrence considered this.

I suppose they do in novels. In the Victorian ones that David loves so much.

'Lawrence!' David yelled, thinking his friend was getting distracted.

Mam was shrieking again. She looked wildly at David. 'Who *is* this bloke, David?'

David swallowed. 'He's – he's...'

'He's your friend, it's fine,' Mam said.

More than that, really.

'Yes,' David agreed. 'More than that.'

I'm his Novelizor.

Mam couldn't really get the gist of what they were on about since she couldn't stop howling. 'What?!'

'Never mind that,' said David, steeling himself. 'It's about time I told you, Mam...'

'AAAGGGHHHH!'

'I'm...'

Mam screamed at him: 'Can we leave this till later?' Then she lapsed into a frantic burst of panting.

Lawrence stepped in, speaking as calmly as he could.

Breathe, Mrs David's-Mam!

Mam tried her best to breathe properly.

In the relatively peaceful pause, David spoke up. 'I'm gay, Mam. That's what.'

'What…?' said Mam. And then she was wracked by another wave of pain that had her screaming fit to burst.

Push, I think, Lawrence told her. I believe this is the time for pushing.

'Did you hear, Mam?' shouted David. 'What I said? I'm gay.'

Mam screamed back at him, through gritted teeth: 'I already knew!'

'What?!'

'Mothers always know!'

Then her screams reached a crescendo, and pretty soon after that, the ambulance arrived again at their door.

*

At the hospital, David and Lawrence found a coffee machine and drank soupy lattes. Then they had Twixes and Twirls – splitting them to be fair – so both had half a Twix and half a Twirl, and Lawrence decided they were the very best kind of food he had eaten since arriving on planet Earth.

'What if she's not all right, Lawrence?'

She will be. Lawrence was sure.

'What if they both die and it's all my fault?'

Lawrence was amazed how long and complicated this human childbirth could be to accomplish.

'Stop pretending that you're not human!' David was glad that the waiting room was empty apart from them.

But I'm not, David! I'm not human. I'm here with a very particular job to do, and I've already compromised that.

'Whatever.'

Do you want to hear how Novelizers are born on Verbatim 6?

'Not especially.'

'We begin as the merest inkling, and then someone says…'

'Listen!'

Suddenly there was all this noise of doors opening and closing, and a baby crying. A nurse appeared before them. David and his Novelizor were gently asked to enter a room, from which the most unearthly racket could be heard…

*

'Come on, don't be shy…' Mam said. 'Say hello to your baby sister.'

David peered close at the little bundle. 'Oh. Wow.' He stared at the bright pink face, squidged shut. It was easy to believe the baby was already having her own thoughts inside that tiny head.

Lawrence took a long, thoughtful look at the baby, too.

She has really long feet.

'She's amazing,' said David.

'Thanks for your help, boys. I'm sorry it was so fraught.'

David was entranced by the baby. Her black scrap of hair, her red fists, which were punching the air, like in triumph.

'I'm calling her Katherine,' Mam announced. 'After your Nanna, even though I hate the blummin' woman.'

David nodded. 'Lovely.'

'Pick her up. Don't be scared.'

David did as he was told. He lifted the baby so carefully. 'She's heavy!'

Mam laughed. 'Tell me about it.'

David held the baby up to Lawrence, too.

Greetings, small human. Greetings from Verbatim 6.

'Ha!' sighed Mam. 'What's he like?'

'He's hilarious.' David rolled his eyes. Then he said, more quietly: 'I texted Dad. Just so he knows…'

'I wish you hadn't.' Then she glanced at him again, curious. 'Any reply yet?'

David shook his head. 'Not yet... but he's probably at work. I'm sure he'll come by later...'

'I'm not sure I want him to.'

'But look at her,' said David. 'Look at Katherine. He's missing all of this.'

'He walked out. We've got our own lives to get on with. And you've got yours, too. With your university stuff.'

'That can wait. I'll take a gap year, or something; stay and help with the baby.'

'Don't you dare!' Mam said crossly. 'I might be what they call an 'older mother' but I'm not geriatric.'

'We'll see.'

'It's your life, David. You have to make sure you live it.'

He chuckled. 'Is this the gas and air talking?'

'I mean it. You do what you want to with your life. And if you do, I'll feel I've done a good job of bringing you up right. And it's true, you know.'

'What is?'

Mam met his stare. 'I already knew about you.'

'Oh, right.'

'About being a puff.'

'Let's talk about it later.'

'I like him. That daft lad. Your boyfriend. That's what he is, isn't he? He's a bit odd, I suppose, with the way he goes on.'

Lawrence was only half listening. He was busy trying to communicate with the newly-born human.

David said awkwardly, 'Well, he's not really my... my...'

'I think he is, you know,' said Mam decisively. 'Now go on, take him home. Get some rest.'

David smiled. 'Thanks, Mam.'

As they left the hospital and went out into the cold to catch the early morning bus, Lawrence was dwelling on the thought that he was now far too close to his subject.

Boyfriend. It was a strange word. Wrong, somehow. But nice. Nicer than 'Novelizor'.

*

A familiar Ford Mondeo pulled up at the bus stop in front of them.

Dad called out of the window, 'Hey, lads!'

'Dad, what are you doing here?'

'You yourself texted me with the news...'

'I never thought you'd come.' It was freezing out on the pavement. Dad had Simply Red playing on his car stereo again.

He said heavily, 'I literally still care about you both, you know.'

Lawrence beamed at him.

Thank you, Mr David's-Dad!

'Not you, daft lad.'

David told his dad, 'She's sleeping now. But she's got a little girl.'

'Lovely.'

She has extremely long feet, Lawrence pointed out.

'Still got your mate with you, I see,' Dad sighed.

'He's not just a mate, Dad,' said David, with sudden resolution. What did he have to lose? 'He's my boyfriend.'

'Oh!' said Dad, taking this in. He looked at them both and went slightly pink. 'Right! I see.' He nodded. 'Well, I guess you'll both be wanting a lift home, yeah?'

*

Twenty minutes later Dad dropped them off and the boys went straight upstairs to David's room. It was early morning and everything was very quiet and still.

Lawrence watched as his friend and subject flung himself down on the bed.

'I could do with a hug,' said David, softly.

Novelizors from Verbatim 6 aren't really trained to give hugs.

'Just give me a hug, will you?'

There were a few moments of rustling then, as Lawrence lay down awkwardly on the bed. They tried to work out who was lying on top of the duvet and who was getting under. David pulled off his jumper and shirt and, after a moment of hesitation, unzipped and shucked off his jeans. Lawrence watched all of this, wondering whether he ought to get undressed too. He wasn't sure what the protocol was. In the end he lay down stiffly, fully-dressed, on top of the duvet, quite close to David. He could smell the milky coffee on his warm breath.

You've got a little sister.

'I know. It's amazing.'

Lawrence thought about that for a bit. Still, your planet is horribly over-populated. I hope your mother puts a stop to her reproductive urges now.

David shoved his shoulder. 'Can't you drop the space act now?'

The what?

'The space act: saying you're from space.' David looked straight into his face and Lawrence felt uncomfortable for a few seconds. 'It's like a neurotic thing. A way of deflecting attention somehow, away from who you really are...'

But this is who I really am.

'Oh – if you can't be serious about anything...'

I *am* serious. This is as serious as it gets.

'No, it isn't...' David smiled at him. Suddenly he felt daring and conscious of all the covers between them. 'Come here.'

They kissed.

It took several hot moments and a few delicate manoeuvres.

Oh.

'Wow,' David whispered. It was like they were in a bubble of secrecy. 'That was my first kiss. I've never...'

Yes. Um.

'Is that all you have to say about it?'

Um.

'You!' David laughed, but he was becoming slightly annoyed too. 'You're never lost for words! You never shut up! Now look at you.'

Er, yes.

'Is that it..?'

Lawrence realized that they had crossed a line. This had gone too far.

'What are you on about?!'

Lawrence was seized by a sudden idea. He sat up in the bed. 'Come with me, David. There's something I want you to see…'

*

Minutes later David was fully dressed again and they both had their coats and shoes on again. They were out in the early morning light, hurrying together over the rubble and rough terrain of the building site.

Lawrence was leading the way to the edge of town and the wasteland.

'What are we doing out here?' David shouted at him.

Come on, and don't ask questions.

'It's the crack of dawn, Lawrence.' David was stumbling over heaps of bricks and sand and scrubby plants.

Maybe it was a mistake to come out like this but the Novelizor had been seized by this sudden, mad impulse.

'When you said you had something to show me…!'

Sssh. This is secret.

Eventually they came to a halt. Lawrence waved his arms about and they stood stock still. Then Lawrence crouched down in the undergrowth and David joined him. Lawrence started pushing aside the overgrown vegetation.

'There's nothing here,' said David. 'What are you looking for?'

I'm going to prove to you, once and for all, who and what I am.

'You don't have to,' David told him. 'You're Lawrence. That's all I need to know...'

We've gone this far. I might as well show you everything.

'Lawrence. It – it...'

He could hear it before he saw it. There was a wonderful chiming noise that filled the morning air. Then there was all this multi-coloured light glittering about and all at once, something appeared before them. Something that was as big as a council house, that hadn't been there a moment before. It was a grand and futuristic vision.

David stared at the rainbow lights at the heart of the waste ground.

'What... what is it?'

My spacecraft. It's been hiding in hyperspace. Sort of tangential to this dimension, you see. Here but not here. I thought it was time to show you. What do you think?

'I... I don't know what to say.'

I used to know the future. I thought I knew how you'd react...

'It's magnificent.'

They're quite common, where I come from, but this one... this one is *mine*.

As if on cue, as if responding to the pride in Lawrence's tone, a hatchway opened in the side of the ship and a shining ramp extended to meet them.

'It's opening...' gasped David. 'Does that mean... Are you..?'

I don't know how things are going to turn out any more. For the first time ever – I don't know the end of the story!

A louder bass note accompanied the chiming noise. It sounded very much as if strange and powerful engines were gearing themselves up.

Lawrence the Novelizor turned to his subject.

Will you come with me, David?

'Uh...' David was flabbergasted. 'Where to?'

Into space. It's all true– everything I said. I come from your future. I fell in love with your books.

'My books?' This brought David up short. His *books?*

They were why I came to this place to find you. All this way. I was meant to just observe, but then I changed things and we kissed and now... will you come with me?

'I write books?! What are they called?'

I can't tell you.

'But... what do I write about?'

All kinds of things. Time. Friendship. Love. How to keep people together. Learning to love them.

'And you want me to leave Earth?'

Will you?

David had to think hard about this.

'Lawrence, my family need me. I've got a new sister. And my mam gets panic attacks when she can't get a supermarket trolley through the revolving doors. And I write books, do I..? And I get... I get *published..?*'

Fully-activated, the semi-sentient ship from Verbatim 6 began to signal its readiness to depart.

I've said too much already, David. We shouldn't even really be in the same story. I used to know how it all worked out. The future was set. But I got too involved.

David took hold of him. 'I do want to go with you, Lawrence. But I can't. I've got to stay here. I've got stuff to do in this world...'

But you can write in space... just think what you might see out there!

'I have to stay. For Mam. And Katherine… Besides, you said you loved my books. If I'm not here to write them, then you'll never read them, and you won't come back to see me, will you? We'd never have met.'

Lawrence knew that he had messed things up. Now everything had changed.

David shook his head. 'Do you know what? I reckon it all changed when you first gave me that journal.'

The ship's noise and brightly-shining lights were intensifying now, as if it was eager for the off.

Lawrence made you want to write?

'You did. Mission accomplished, I reckon.'

But I was sent to observe…! Not to change your life…

'But you have!' David grinned. 'You've changed it, forever, I think.'

It's only been a couple of weeks…

'Maybe that's enough.' David hugged Lawrence hard, and felt him relax into it at last. 'Will you come back then? One day?'

If I can. I will. I promise.

Then Lawrence kissed David, and stepped away.

Goodbye, David.

'Goodbye, Lawrence. I'm really going to miss you...' David had to shout to be heard over the spaceship engine noises. 'And thank you!'

For what?

'You've read my books – you tell me!'

Lawrence turned and hurried away into his beloved ship. David watched as the ramp slid back and the hatchway smoothly closed. Then the ship seemed to glow in a satisfied kind of way before lifting off, gloriously, into the brightening air of the morning.

*

Home again, later, David went back to writing in his journal.

When I turned seventeen I didn't really know who I was, or what I might become.

And then, all of a sudden, I *did*.

I knew exactly who I was.

And I knew who it was I was writing for.

And I knew that, when he read it, he would love my story.

The Middle of Nowhere

I remember living in a square house beside a lake and a concrete bridge.

It was just Mam and me. I was a good talker and she said I was good company. Dad was away a lot and eventually he stopped coming back altogether.

We lived in a square box on an estate of square boxes. Mam said we lived in the middle of nowhere, but that was okay with her.

When I was little I loved that phrase. 'The middle of nowhere' was what it felt like to stand on that concrete bridge and look at the lake and all the other houses and wonder about them.

*

Every day we went to the shop and we had to go over the bridge across the little lake. There were lazy orange fish down there and tall green reeds. The water seemed to go down forever.

Twice a day we went over that strangely-shaped concrete bridge. It had been designed by a famous architect, Mam said, and that was why it wasn't quite ordinary.

When we went to the shop we'd take a basket round and get just what we needed for each day. A tin of tomato soup, a small loaf of bread, a bottle of milk, a bag of sausage rolls.

By the counter there was a spinning rack of books that went round and round until the covers and titles blurred. The shopkeeper laughed. 'You can't buy him one of those fairy tale books every time you come in! He'll be spoiled!'

'It's my money,' said Mam crossly. She hated being told what she could and couldn't do.

'One day you'll run out of fairy tales,' the shopkeeper warned.

'Then we'll make up our own,' she said.

I was proud of my mam. She looked pretty and had long, shiny brown hair and she dressed very modern. 'You can have a new fairy tale book every time I can afford one,' she told me.

'It's just you and me against the world,' she told me.

*

Every night it was a new story that she read me, and on the days she couldn't afford a new one, we went back to the start and read the old ones again. Or she would try to make one up.

She read aloud to me and I followed the pictures and turned the pages. I was pretending I could read for myself and that the words were coming to make sense.

'One day you'll be able to read to yourself and then you won't need me to sit here with you.'

'I will,' I said.

That night I wasn't sure, but I thought I could hear her crying through the thin walls.

I never understood why she was sad so much of the time. She cried after visits from her family.

*

My Big Nanna came to see us and I liked it then because long ago she had grown up in the countryside and knew the names for all the trees and the birds. She'd point them out when we went for a walk and make me repeat them.

She was a tall woman in a thick sheepskin coat and dyed brown hair.

We crossed the strange bridge over the lake and I said, 'There's a troll who lives under this bridge, Big Nanna. If you don't hurry he comes crawling out and eats little kids like me.'

'What's that?' my Big Nanna gasped. 'What nonsense!'

'It's true, Big Nanna,' I told her. I wanted her to feel the same lovely fear that I felt, going over that bridge. 'And in that water there's a dragon. When he breathes fire he turns all the water to steam, and he gobbles up old women like you!'

My Big Nanna pursed her lips. 'Don't be so cheeky.'

When we got home with the day's shopping she said to Mam, 'I don't know what you've been filling his head with.'

'Fairy tales,' said Mam. She was lying on the settee, under a duvet. She wasn't feeling well and that was why Big Nanna was staying overnight. She was helping out.

'Fairy tales?' my Big Nanna snapped. 'But he's a little boy.'

'I read them to him every night,' said Mam. 'And when we run out, we try to make up our own. And soon he'll be able to read for himself.'

I took my Big Nanna to my room and showed her the bookcase. The top shelf had a sliding glass window. Behind this, pride of place, was my fairy tale collection.

'This isn't the kind of thing little boys like,' said my Big Nanna.

But still, while Mam was ill, Big Nanna read to me. That night and then the next. She didn't do all the proper voices for the characters, though she tried.

*

When we went to the shop I told Big Nanna: 'There's an old wizard who lives on this bridge. In the shadows over there. Can you hear him?'

'You're being fanciful,' she said. 'Stop it!'

'And down in that darkest bit underneath the bridge,' I went on. 'There's a magic dog with eyes as big as tea plates.'

'What?' cried Big Nanna, who was scared of big dogs. 'Where is he? What..?!'

'And if you jump on his back he'll fly you many miles away. As far away as Dad lives now.'

My Big Nanna frowned and told me I had to stop making things up. People didn't like it when kids got cheeky and started lying. 'Your mam's not well with her nerves. Do you really want her worrying about you getting into trouble?'

I decided not to tell Big Nanna about any of the other stuff I was thinking about.

After midday she was going home to her own town on the bus. It was her bingo afternoon. The bus stop was just outside our house, so I was allowed to stand with her waiting. 'Now, just you be good for your mam,' she said. I watched her climb aboard and I waved her off.

'You're a good boy, seeing your Big Nanna off like that,' said my mam from her place on the settee.

'A giant bird flew down from the clouds and seized her in its claws and carried her away,' I said. 'Then it ate her.'

'Oh, good,' said Mam.

*

The next day it was raining. Our estate was miserable and dark. All the lights glowed yellow in the middle of the day. Mam felt well enough for us to walk to the shop. We both fitted under her umbrella.

'There's a witch living under this bridge,' I said. 'She eats dragonflies and wine gums and drinks so much lemonade you can hear her burping if you listen very carefully. But if she catches you crossing her bridge she turns you into…' I squeezed Mam's hand. 'What does she turn you into?'

'Hmm,' she thought. 'Let's see. A packet of fish fingers?'

'Fish fingers!' I laughed. 'Yes!'

She'd made that one up before, ages ago. It was brilliant that she remembered it.

At the shop she counted up her money for the day's groceries and said, 'No extra pennies today. I'm sorry.'

I was spinning the book rack round. I had my eye on the story about the old lady who knitted the endless magic scarf. But it blurred in with the others as the rack sped up.

Mam was cross all the way home, like she was the one who really wanted that new story.

*

The next day my Aunty Sandra turned up. She was Mam's older sister. She threw off her damp fur coat and sighed. 'You aren't really ill. You've got yourself stuck in a rut, looking at the same four walls. No wonder you're fed up. You're in the middle of nowhere with a kid.'

Mam didn't say much.

When it came to the shopping Aunty Sandra was like, 'I'm not taking the kid with me.' She rolled her eyes. 'Look, why don't I just whiz up the road in my car to the Superstore and load you up with a month's worth of groceries? I could fill your empty cupboards.'

Mam shook her head. 'That's not how we do it. And he likes going over the lake and the bridge to the little shop.'

So Aunty Sandra took me over the bridge and the lake to the shop, borrowing Mam's umbrella.

As we crossed the bridge I told her, 'There's a giant bat who sometimes comes to visit the troll who lives under this bridge and they eat licorice together until their tongues turn black.'

'Yeah, yeah, kid,' said Aunty Sandra, starting to walk faster. 'I haven't got all day.'

She filled her basket with what she called 'proper nutritious food. None of that convenience muck your mother always buys.'

While Aunty Sandra queued at the checkout I turned the paperback rack round and round. I stopped though when I realized she might think I was hinting and asking for a book.

She came struggling over with four full plastic bags. 'Can you give me a hand?' she snapped. 'You're a big boy now and you can help. What are you looking at there?'

'Fairy tales,' I told her.

She gasped. 'Boys don't like fairy tales.' She led me to the rack of comics and chose one about football players. 'That's the kind of thing a boy like you should like.'

Then we walked home, back across the estate. When we came to the lake and the bridge I said, 'Mam says there's a hairy yeti who lives over in one of those houses. She said when he gets mad his temper is abominable...'

Aunty Sandra tutted. 'Where are you getting all this stuff from? You and your mother are crazy.'

That night we had to watch TV shows that my aunty liked. They were quiz shows in which people won cash prizes for guessing answers. When bedtime came I had to read my football comic. 'No, I won't read it to you. Just look at the pictures,' said Aunty Sandra.

*

The next day Aunty Sandra was off.

'I've done my bit of helping. I don't believe you're ill at all. I don't believe in nerves, as it happens. I just think you're miserable, because you've got yourself stuck in the middle of nowhere with a kid.'

Aunty Sandra patted me on the head and put on her fake fur coat. Then she zoomed off in her car in the direction of the motorway.

Mam said, 'I'll try to get up tomorrow. Don't worry. We'll be okay.'

And she did. The sun came out and all the green rushes and lily pads in the lake were a brilliant green. Mam put on her new coat she'd bought in the sales and together we crossed the bridge. She told me that sometimes a princess came and stood on the top of the bridge and wondered which of the frogs below might actually be a prince. 'And, do you know, it was all of them? And she had a huge problem picking out her favourite one? In the end she didn't bother and just let them carry on being frogs.'

We went to the shop and the shopkeeper was so pleased to see her. She bought fish fingers and sliced white bread and tomato ketchup so we could have fish finger sandwiches for tea. And she said, 'I've kept back exactly enough to buy a fairy tale book.'

I found the one about the woman who knitted the magical endless scarf. It was one of the few listed on the back covers that I didn't have.

On the way home though, Mam had a funny turn. That was what Big Nanna called it afterwards.

*

'You understand, don't you?' Big Nanna asked me. 'She might have seemed to be getting better, but she wasn't really. She's always been bad with her nerves. And now we all have to care for her.'

'But I do. I do!' I wanted to say. 'I always care for her! She's the most important person in the world.'

Then my Big Nanna had to go home, but she sent her youngest daughter to stay with us. My Aunty Shelley.

In some ways it was great because Aunty Shelley believed in eating sweets in bed and drinking pop for breakfast and doing just what you wanted to most of the time.

Best of all, when we went over the bridge and I told her stories, she believed every word.

She had frizzy hair and a long orange coat that swirled around her.

'Wait here,' she told me, and crept up onto the bridge by herself. Then all at once she was screaming and shouting and saying that the dragon had caught hold of her and wouldn't let her go. 'Have you got the magic sword?' she screeched at me.

'Yes! Yes!' I shouted, dashing up the concrete steps.

'Then you have to lop off his head!' yelled Aunty Shelley.

Which I did easily, of course. The dragon's head flew clear through the air and landed in the lake with a great splash.

'Hooray!' cried Aunty Shelley.

*

The days of Aunty Shelley staying with us didn't last for long, but they were great while they did. She invented sugar sandwiches.

That's where you butter the bread and sprinkle sugar and then shake it over the sugar bowl but most of the sugar sticks. Just like making a picture with glitter and glue. The sugar crunches and sparkles when you bite into it. Mam was horrified: 'You'll rot all the teeth right out of your head.'

Aunty Shelley also invented the game where you go to the top of that steep hill on the way into town and run down it as fast as you can. I was used to Mam taking it so carefully in her stack-heeled boots. When I'd been in my pushchair we'd crept up and down that hill ever so gingerly. But now it was autumn and the leaves were drifting thick.

'All the colours! I just want to fling myself into all those colours, don't you?' Aunty Shelley seized my hand and we ran full pelt down the hill. Of course we tripped and slipped and rolled all the way down to the bottom, sending up flurries of beautiful leaves.

When Big Nanna saw us one time she was horrified. 'There'll be dog's muck under there. You'll be rolling in dog's muck! You mark my words!'

But Aunty Shelley just laughed at her. She laughed in her face. She hardly ever took anything seriously.

Maybe Mam felt a bit left out. She was stronger and getting up and about more, but she was tired a lot of the time, and couldn't join in as much as she'd like to.

She came to the play park with us and sat on the bench, wrapped up against the whipping wind. But Aunty Shelley was running around the park with me. She didn't care if she looked silly climbing up the slide or whirling around on the Witch's Hat. She pretended she was there to keep an eye on me, but I knew she was glad of the excuse to play on all the rides.

I'd never seen anyone swing so high. It was like she was going up to the very top. It was almost like she was going to right round in a circle. It was dangerous. Mam shouted up at her, but she just laughed.

Walking home Mam reminded her about something that happened when they were kids. 'Remember? When we used to jump on the bus?'

Aunty Shelley looked mystified for a moment. She looked like she didn't remember anything longer than about a week ago.

Mam told the story. She walked along beside us, sighing and shaking her head, but she laughed a couple of times too. It was about how when they were girls they had this craze for jumping onto the bus when it was moving, rather than waiting at the bus stop and getting on like anyone normal did. Instead they waited for it going by and then they'd run after it and take a running jump at the little platform thing at the back, with the pole that the conductor sometimes hung onto.

I stared at Mam, trying to imagine her doing something as dangerous and naughty as that.

'I was a good runner and I was good at gymnastics,' said Mam. 'When I was nine I was, anyway. So I'd always manage it easy. I'd fly through the air and land on the bus and grab that pole. Sometimes the conductor would tell us off, but it was always worth it.'

'I think I remember this,' Aunty Shelley says. 'Are you talking about the time when I almost fell off?'

Mam laughed. 'But you didn't! You almost missed, but you grabbed that pole and you hung on for dear life, but your legs gave out, and you were dragged along the road...'

Aunty Shelley was laughing too now, though to me it sounded horribly scary. 'And it was all down to our dad!' she burst out. 'Wasn't it? Right at the last second, just before I ran and jumped... I saw him! He was coming down the street on the other side. He'd caught us doing this stupid thing! And he whipped his hat off and waved it about, trying to get my attention... And that's why I jumped wrong and ended up getting dragged along...'

They were both laughing helplessly now, thinking about their dad being so furious with them, and how horrified he was, seeing Aunty Shelley getting dragged along by the bus.

'It only lasted a few seconds till the bus stopped again,' laughed Aunty Shelley. 'But it was the most terrifying few seconds of my life. And he went mad with us, didn't he, when he came running up..?'

'He walloped us both,' Mam agreed.

'He hit you?' I gasped.

'He was frightened and worried,' Aunty Shelley said. 'We were daft kids. We didn't know what danger was.'

'I've never really told you much about my dad,' Mam said to me. We carried on walking towards the town centre. She was definitely feeling stronger, if we were going as far as the precinct. 'He would have been your granddad. But he died when me and your Aunty Shelley were just kids. You would have loved him, just like we did. He was lovely, wasn't he, Shelley?'

'Oh, yes,' said my Aunty. 'I remember him really well. And he'd have loved this little man, too. He'd be so proud of you.'

Catskin

Catskin was a boy – not a girl, like the old tale has it. Also, his father – who was a rich land-owner – craved a daughter, not a son, and so he was greatly disappointed in the hero of our story. 'What good are boys?' he sneered. 'Nasty, galumphing, dirty, brutish things.' And the ghost of his wife – who'd died in childbirth – quite agreed.

The father told Catskin he'd have to go off and find his own fortune.

At great expense a wicked fairy was summoned up to fetch the gifts he would need:

A cloak woven from the feathers of the rarest birds in all the kingdom. This would let him travel swiftly, as far away from home as possible.

A gown sewn from silk produced by the most slippery and changeable spinning beasts known to man. This dress would give the boy the appearance of a beautiful girl: something he would find very handy, the wicked fairy said.

Lastly came the gift that gave the boy his name, after eighteen years of being called nothing but 'You, boy.' The fairy was wicked indeed and thought nothing of catching and skinning a dozen cats from the town. Gleefully she stitched their pelts into a multi-coloured, rank-smelling suit complete with furry ears and whiskers. It was Catskin's curse to wear this every day.

The wicked fairy hated the sight of the gangly boy almost as much as his father did.

'Then I shall go,' said Catskin and, without further ado, hurried out of his father's home and out of the lands his father owned. His father was too busy kissing the wicked fairy – locked in her enchanted embrace – to even notice.

Catskin bounded through the forest, possessed by the stolen vigour of a dozen stray moggies. When he rested high up in the trees at night their screechy voices haunted him:

Yooouuu can live ooouuur lives
Yowwww yowwwwww
Yoooowww Yoowwwwwww
Youuuu can live oooooouuuur lives!

He travelled far afield, donning the cloak of exotic feathers and visiting many kingdoms, and all kinds of adventures were his. He grew wily and powerful and yet his heart still yearned for someone of his own to love.

At last it came about that he was working as a scullery boy in the filthy kitchens of a palace in a kingdom far away from home.

'Work harder, Catskin. We've chickens to broil and chips to fry and a thousand bottles of wine to open before the ball tonight,' said the lazy cook, who sat each night by the fire drinking, preferring to let Catskin do all the work. It was the week when three glorious balls were held in the palace and there was plenty of work to do.

'I'd like to go to those balls,' Catskin thought, as he peeled potatoes and turned pullets on spits and filled vol-au-vent cases. He spied from the castle windows as guests arrived in carriages and helicopters.

One was a Prince, and the finest Prince ever seen thereabouts. At the very sight of him the boy found himself growing warm inside his snug and by-now rather dirty Catskin.

When he asked the cook if he could go to the ball that night the cook laughed and beat him with a heavy mixing bowl.

But Catskin crept out in the moonlight, just as the band was striking up in that glitzy ballroom. He ran to the woods and the hollow tree where he had hidden his only possessions. He stripped off his Catskin and bathed naked in a nearby pool, loving that coolness of the water on his skin.

Then he dressed in the gown of strange silk and he returned to the palace.

At the ball everyone wondered at the sight of this incredibly beautiful young woman. The Prince almost fell over at the sight of her. They dallied. They danced. They kissed and they fooled around a little in the pleasure gardens. When dawn came up the Prince cried out, for the girl had disappeared.

Catskin was racing back to the woods, where he exchanged his finery for his catskin, knowing he must be back in the kitchens in order to begin cooking all the breakfasts. There were a lot of visitors that week, and a lot of eggs to fry.

The cook could barely look at him, since he was so thick-headed and hungover. He didn't even notice Catskin's cheeriness as he carried out his chores. Under his catskin the boy was glowing with the memory of a prince's kisses.

'Do you think I might attend the second ball?' he asked the cook.

The cook took up a heavy metal pan and beat him with it. 'Of course not, you idiot!'

Above stairs everyone was hearing about the Prince's raised hopes. Where was this beautiful girl? Where had she fled to? How might they find her?

Would she return for the second ball of the week?

Indeed, that very night, Catskin waited till the cook was dead drunk and snoring and the band was launching into their first number and all the lanterns were lit ready for another night of partying, and then he dashed off into the woods again.

Once more he ran to the tree with the hollow and divested himself of his catskin. He shivered with anticipated pleasure as he bathed in the water of the forest pool. And then he took out – not the silken gown – but the cloak of exotic feathers, and wrapped it about himself, pulling the cowl around his face.

He returned to the palace and marched brazenly into the midst of the party.

Heads turned. Fans were stilled. Whispers went rippling through the gaudy rooms.

The Prince – alerted as if by a sixth sense – turned to see a stranger wrapped in a feathery cloak striding towards him. His heart started to pound inside his royal breast. Now, this wasn't the girl from last night, was it..? And yet... and yet...

They dallied. They danced. They laughed and they talked and they dallied again. And then they kissed and they fooled around in the moonlit gardens and lo and behold it seemed this really was the same person the Prince had met last night.

He was tired and dozed on the dewy grass and – alas – he found that the lad was gone once more.

Catskin, of course, was back at his stove, cooking breakfast.

'It's the last of the balls tonight,' the cook taunted him. 'Are you still dreaming about hobnobbing with your betters?'

'Yes, I am,' said Catskin.

The cook picked up a wooden ladle and went to beat him with it. 'Such things aren't for the likes of us!'

But Catskin snatched the ladle from the cook and cracked him across the skull with it. 'There,' he said. 'I've been meaning to do that.'

Then he returned to his tasks, looking forward keenly to the final party of the week.

That evening he sent up the decanters of wine and the trays of canapés and all the rest of it, and the lamps were lit and the music began. And word went round that the Prince was much more desperate than ever to learn the identity of the boy – or was it a girl? Or was it a girl pretending to be a boy? – with whom he had dallied and fooled around during the previous two nights.

Catskin smiled to himself.

He went to the woods and he peeled off his skin and bathed luxuriously. But this time he put his catskin back on and preened his whiskers. He walked back into the palace through the main entrance.

People drew back and gasped and clutched their pearls. Who was this furry, savage-looking beast?

'I am Catskin,' he told the Prince, and took his hand.

'Are you?' asked the Prince, staring hard into his eyes. 'Is that who you truly are?'

Voices rang out. 'It's a monster! It's a creature! It's a nonesuch beast! Throw it out immediately!'

One of the serving maids screamed. The butler called the cook, who came swaying drunkenly into the ballroom, rubbing his eyes. 'Why, it's the serving boy!' he bellowed. 'It's Catskin! What the devil is he doing here..?'

Well... he was dallying with the Prince. And then they were dancing and laughing and dancing again and then, just before dawn, they were kissing and fooling around in the moonlit gardens.

Everyone simply stared at all these goings-on.

The next day they went off in the Prince's carriage and they travelled all the way to Catskin's own land, where they sought out the father who had spurned him. Having been cheated and fleeced by the wicked fairy, the old man now had nothing but a poky little shack to live in. He also had a terrible one-eyed witch for a companion. He was full of regrets and sobbed loudly when he saw his son again and the fine Prince who was now so deeply in love with him.

The one-eyed witch was called Betsy 'Must Dash' Moustache on account of her curious coiled-up moustache and the fact she never stayed in one place for very long. 'Your father is a complete arse,' she told Catskin. 'Lovely lad like you. Fancy chucking you out! Still, you've done well for yourself, haven't you? What a splendid Prince you've found! Now, what about that magic frock and that enchanted cloak – will you be needing them? Or will you give them to Betsy, LOL?'

Catskin was so utterly loved up and crazy about his Prince that he forgave his arse of a father for everything, and he also let Betsy 'Must Dash' Moustache steal away with his gown and his cloak.

And that was the beginning of the story of all the trouble Betsy caused with those extremely valuable garments.

But in the mean time those boys – Catskin and the Prince – lived very happily ever after.

The TV Writer

Manchester 1995

He just loved television, and always had done.

When he was little it was mostly just Ian and his dad. Dad worked very close to home. He was a carpenter and an all-round odd-job man. He was there each lunch time when Ian came home from school and they would watch anything that was on. Usually shows with puppets or soaps about hospitals or Australia. They were the same in the evening, eating their tea off trays on their knees, tuning into the latest quiz shows and sit-coms. It didn't matter what came on, really. They watched everything and they watched it together.

Perhaps they could have talked to each other more. They didn't even talk about the programmes they viewed. Anyone looking in from the outside would remark on their lack of communication right away. There was a lack of understanding between them, perhaps. Dad with his oily hands and that smell of wood shavings and glue. Ian sitting there, all particular, in the tidy way he dressed himself. He'd always been very smart. It was almost strange.

The two of them had no idea what went on in each other's heads. But that had always been true, going back to the time that Ian's mum was still living with them. That didn't necessarily mean there was a lack of warmth or love in their lives. Ian's dad just didn't talk much. He never had. And Ian always felt safe and secure at home. He felt loved in that house from the moment he woke up in the morning and could hear breakfast telly already droning away in the kitchen. He felt the same way last thing at night when he fell asleep to the muffled noise of gunfire and screaming of the late night movies.

His dad was proud but bemused when Ian went to work in Manchester at the TV studios. He was twenty-two when he got the call. They wanted to see him. The drama department wanted to interview him. There was a possible job waiting for him down in Manchester.

Now, there hadn't been anything said about it, but twenty-two was pretty old for thinking about getting a proper job. Ian had worked shifts in the shop on their estate, and odd hours behind the bar in his dad's local. His dad didn't like him working there, having heard his son described as a puff and whatnot. Seeing him at the bar pulling pints had made his dad look at him differently, from afar. And yeah, maybe he was a puff or something. But they didn't talk about it. And maybe his son would be better off getting a job somewhere else, in a more cosmopolitan place? A job with better prospects.

A job on the telly, though. That was mind-boggling.

Ian had grown up in Sunderland, which seemed a world away for a lad who'd never been anywhere.

Dad didn't quite understand why the telly people wanted to see his son. He read the letter again and again. 'But how do they even know who you are, bonny lad?' He looked so perplexed. It was like he thought those TV people had been watching them, all those nights, from the other side of the screen. They had noticed how entranced Ian was by everything he saw.

And he really was. Ian could give all his attention to the telly. He'd sit in front of any old crap. So long as the talking heads were slightly larger than life-sized, and the colours were brighter and the voices came booming out of the hidden speakers in the corner of the room.

At school his mind wandered like anything. He walked down the street like he was in a constant daze. People thought he had something wrong with him, like he was backward or deaf. But he was fine. He was just thinking about soap characters and plots and everything that he imagined happening next, or in scenes that never got broadcast. His whole imaginative life was about dwelling on the future and the promise and allure of endless episodes to come.

When the competition had been announced in the TV Times he entered as if he really had no choice. He never said anything about it. There was no need. He was never going to actually win, of course. Millions of people sent entries into contests like this, didn't they? His chances were slim, but there was no stopping him. He wrote his sit-com one Christmas holiday, caught in the grip of a strange compulsion.

Write the first episode of your very own comedy show. Make it about anything you like.

He stopped working so much at the pub. He turned down extra hours. His dad started thinking he was depressed. He was having a crisis of some kind. Maybe he'd come downstairs wanting to talk. His dad lived in dread of him coming down and wanting to have the gay talk, or telling him he was on drugs. Or worst of all, maybe he wanted to be a woman now. His dad kept watching the telly and tried to block this stuff out.

But Ian was typing away on a computer his dad had bought to help his handyman business, but he had failed to get the hang of it.

Ian was writing his sit-com. He called it 'Hilarity Ensues.'

It was so hard. It all took so long. He wanted to cry with frustration.

He had never realized before how long half an hour could really be.

While he was grinding his teeth and printing out immaculate pages only to rip them up again, and making himself sick with instant coffee and cudgeling his brains till they felt like cookie dough it suddenly struck him that maybe he stood a better chance at winning this than he had at first supposed. Not because he was writing a script of unmitigated genius but because who else, really, would go to all this effort? Who else was going to be arsed to write and type out a whole thirty minute script? This wasn't like coming up with a catchy slogan for cornflakes, or a trivia question you could answer in a flash. This was work. It was frigging hard work.

So he cheered up at once, finished off his script during the frosty days before New Year, printed it all out and posted the bastard thing to Manchester. A brown manilla envelope. The distillaton of twenty years of watching everything with Dad. Then he tried to put it out of his mind.

It didn't win but two months later they informed him he'd come fourth, and they wanted to invite him to Granada Studios anyway. They wanted him to meet the brightest and best of their producers and script editors, who were always on the lookout for exciting new talent and that, apparently, was what Ian was.

*

They were very nice to him, he supposed.

He looked skinny, fresh-faced, gangly and nervous. His smartest clothes were rumpled from the train journey. He'd spent hours getting to Manchester and it was his first time on a train. He'd seen an actress who played a major role in the studio's most famous soap at Piccadilly Station and so he felt a bit star-struck and daft as soon as he arrived. He knew he needed to be cooler about things.

It was a blocky building with hundreds of narrow offices and an iconic red sign on its roof. The tall windows looked out on dingy orange Victorian warehouses and the glitz of theatres and fancy stores.

He sat in full glaring sunlight as one of the two men he was meeting gabbled away almost without pause.

'Your years at university were completely wasted. I never went to university and neither did Bill, did you Bill? And look at us now. I'm twenty-five and I'm producing my second show. Not going to college has never held me back. I've never got into debt and studied something completely irrelevant, I've just got straight on with what I really want to do. All I needed to know about is making telly, isn't that right, Bill?'

The producer's burlier friend, Bill the script editor, smiled from behind his computer and nodded.

'It's like...' Kevin the producer went on. 'When I talk to writers and script editors and directors and you ask them, what do you think is wrong with this script? And they flummox and flounder and they try to tell you all this complicated stuff and it's all just excuses. They over-intellectualise everything. I just go, 'No! Stop! I'll tell you what's wrong with the thing. It's-just-frigging-boring! That's all what it is! I don't feel *drawn in by* it! I don't frigging care enough for what's going on! It might all be very clever-clever and erudite and all about the research that's gone into it, but if I don't *feel* that actual human connection with the characters then it isn't worth anything! You might as well take all the pages and wipe your arse with them."

The three of them were drinking vile machine coffee out of paper cups. The sun was blinking through Ian's dyed-blonde fringe. While Kevin was ranting on, Ian looked away from the sun and started covertly checking out the folders on the shelves and the labeled VHS tapes stacked everywhere. He was trying his hardest to get his head round it all.

Here he was: in the very place where scripts got read and lines were crossed out and rewritten and it all ended up on the telly. It ended up in Ian and his dad's front room. It all started here. It started as brilliant ideas that people like Kevin handed out to writers, just like it was homework for them to do by a certain date. And when it all came back in the post Kevin would rewrite almost every single word completely and then they'd do it all again and again until it was all exactly right.

Until it was all exactly how Kevin wanted it.

One page represented a minute (Ian had learned this for himself, reading out his script to himself in his room at home) and eventually a script was a neatly-clipped thirty-odd page document, sharp and tidy and perfect. Then it was 'locked down', which meant that no further changes could happen to it, and then it was given to everyone involved in the production, including the actors, who had to learn the whole thing off by heart and then act it all out in poky wooden rooms constructed inside the cavernous studios that lay directly underneath this very building.

Magic.

Ian had known all this stuff – in theory – before getting there that afternoon. But sitting in the office with these two men only slightly older than he was made him feel completely gobsmacked. There was something Olympian about it all.

Now Kevin was becoming manic. 'What I do is, I shake their scripts. I give them a good frigging shaking, every page. That's my secret. And, you see, all the shit falls out. All the rubbishy, useless, irrelevant shit that every writer always tries to put in. Out it all drops and do you know what I'm left with, Ian?'

Ian shook his head dumbly.

'I'm left with the *very essence*. I'm left with the heart of the story and the hearts of the characters. And that's what works on TV. Only the very heart of the thing. The core of the human drama and the conflicts between those people and absolutely no shit whatsoever. Not all the rubbishy crap that writers always pad out their plays with, or that you always get in bloody books and whatever. I'm talking about the essence. The essential essence of the thing.

'That's what all the viewers love. Characters who say exactly what they really mean. Stories that are really about something that every viewer can care about. Do you see? It has to be people and things folk give a shit about. Everything else is a waste of time. And that's what we're after here, me and Bill.

'This is the secret of it all. And it's a secret I've always known. That's my gift, you see. I can see how stories should be told. I know what makes drama tick. And it might sound a tiny bit arrogant to say so, but it's so, so true. I scare the *crap* out of everyone here with my unerring instincts and the way I shout about stuff. But it's only because I'm always right, you see? It's all about knowing how to tell a story properly. Now, I'm frigging famished. Shall we have one of those Chicken Tikka pizzas, Bill? Shall we take the lad out to Pizza Express for lunch?'

Off they went and Ian was just too nervous to eat as he listened to more of this stuff. Their tales of triumph and conquest.

Bill asked him – quietly, in a lull – what his favourite shows were. He couldn't think of a single one.

At the end of lunch Kevin invited him to write an episode of a soap opera they were starting. It was a late night soap, set in a department store and it was to be called 'Menswear.'

This chance was everything Ian had ever wanted.

He realized this at that very moment as they left the pizza place and wandered boozily back to the office.

He was a bit pissed (they had ordered a bottle of Prosecco to celebrate), elated and, of course, shit scared.

*

'*Play the subtext!*'

That's what they kept saying to Ian, all that summer. Kevin the producer used to say it in this needling way, making it a mantra, exaggerating his own Scouse accent.

Ian was never exactly sure what they meant by '*play the subtext*.' The answer seemed to change every time he asked. He only got the right idea about it when it was much too late.

For those few weeks that summer when he could legitimately call himself 'a writer for television' he assumed that the phrase had to do with the need to make everything underground and hidden in the dialogue. All of the motives and the deepest desires of the characters had to be subtly unpacked for the audience. He assumed it was important not to give the game away too quickly or obviously…

In those gloriously hot summer days in the city he made a new pal called Liz, who was a TV writer already. She sat in script meetings with him and they doodled daft messages on each other's pads. They visited the open air set of the country's favourite soap opera together, snapping pictures of each other outside the famous landmarks. She took him to Canal Street and the Gay Village for his first ever visit. They sat on a balcony at Manto's on a roasting hot day, sipping gin and tonics and staring at the cityscape in front of them. A mostly empty car park fringed with ferns and billboards advertising luxury apartments. They watched the seething streets and the murky green of the canal water rushing by.

Liz was a very intense person, Ian was discovering. She'd sit smoking and dragging as hard as she could on every cigarette, till little lines appeared on her forehead. Right now she seemed to be concentrating hard on what Ian was telling her.

'Everyone in real life is so hard to read,' he said. 'I can't tell what any of them are thinking.'

Liz was bundled up in a very stylish pink cardigan Ian knew came from a fancy shop because she had told him so. She wore a vintage minidress she'd picked up in Didsbury Oxfam and her unwashed hair was knotted up like Bjork's. She was pretty stylish.

Ian went on, 'People are deep and complicated. Everyone is. Even people you don't expect to be. Everyone is deep.'

Liz looked at him and shook her head, amazed. 'That's just not true. I always think that everyone's completely see-through. It's easy to see what motivates people. It's usually dead obvious. Money, sex, power, self-interest. Fear. The usual stuff.'

At first Ian thought she was joking.

'I mean it,' she snapped. 'I don't believe in mixed feelings. And I don't believe in psychology. I think all that's fake. People are quite straightforward, really, and anyone telling you different is usually lying or trying to exploit you.'

Ian was way too excited at actually being in the Gay Village with its crowds and seemingly endless parade of café bars and bunting and fairy lights to properly take in what she was telling him.

He should really be listening, he thought. He had a lot to learn not from her insight as such, but from her certainty and her knowledge of how to play the game they were both engaged in.

The part of his mind that was really listening to her words was vaguely aware that he thought she was talking bollocks. Of course people were more complex than she was making out. The whole of life was completely different to how she was describing it. Liz was just cynical, that was it. At the age of thirty she believed that she had everything sorted out and everyone she had ever met pigeonholed and reduced to type.

Ian watched her observing the Saturday night faggots and dykes trundling up and down Canal Street and it was like she was the oldest soul there. She was like some all-seeing deity who had seen it all before and who was bored. An omniscient, omnipotent deity with her hair in bunches and glittery eye make-up on.

'Tiresias in 'The Wasteland,' he mumbled, crunching an ice cube. He had suddenly remembered one of his A level set texts. 'That's who you're like.'

She shrugged. 'I don't know what that is.' She gave him a funny look. 'You waste too much time with books, I know that much. Has it been adapted?'

He was thrilled that this bitter, snappish, skinny woman had decided she was going to be his mate. She would guide him through the many pitfalls of his new life – in this city, this Village, and this whole business of knocking out scripts for TV shows that millions of people would watch…

Liz had written for all the major shows and she was very blasé about it all. She'd even won awards. She had bought a small flat in Castlefield by the canal and put down a deposit on a two-bedroomed terraced house in Hebden Bridge, which was the West Yorkshire town where all the successful Manchester writers dreamed of moving to one day. They longed for the leafy valley half an hour away on the gently chugging train…

Her life, Ian thought, was idyllic. And her certainty about things was the most enviable thing of all. Just like Kevin the producer, she was absolutely sure when things were good and right. She knew when she did good work. It came in a flash, decisively. She didn't have to try too hard. In fact, trying too hard would ruin it.

'You know when you used to draw at school? And you'd get it wrong and try to rub the pencil marks out? And you rub it out again and again and the paper would go grey and nubbly? And then the page would tear? That's what it's like when writers try too hard and too much. It's useless. You just have to know what you're doing. And be quick and accurate and don't frig it about.' She shrugged. She had all the answers. Ian collected them all up. The more he listened, the more they seemed not just to be about the art of writing for TV, but about everything. About life itself. When he suggested this she threw back her head and laughed like a clogged drain.

It wasn't arrogance that made her go on like this, he realized. It was talent. She was talented, young, very sure of herself, and destined for great things.

'Stick with me, kid...' She actually said that to him, during one of those early nights out. She had the rare gift of being able to come out with things that Ian would once have thought of as whopping clichés. The very thought of those phrases would have made him bite them back.

'What's a cliché but the truth?' she said, which he forbade himself from pointing out was a cliché in itself. 'Things are clichés for a reason,' she added sagely.

She knew best, he thought. She knew the answers.

She was his mentor.

After a week or two she said it was ridiculous, his sloping off after every script meeting and going home to Sunderland. Expensive, too. What was the point? His dad could survive without him (could he?) Ian needed to be in the city, being ready for quick turnarounds and lightning edits and emergency meetings at the studios. Also, he needed to be seeing a bit of real life and being a part of it all.

She invited him to stay at her flat in the new developments near Granada. She offered him the fold-out settee in her living room. It was on the ground floor and he was welcome to stay over weekends and accompany her out on the town. They could dance and stay out till dawn if they liked. They could have brunch in the cafes by Deansgate, hungover and sharing tales of their adventures the night before. Then they could shop and spend their hard-earned cash in the increasingly swanky shops that were opening up in the centre of town. Manchester was changing: getting smarter and fancier and Ian simply had no choice in the matter of sharing these changes with Liz.

He didn't need pushing into it, though. He ended up with a kind of crush on her whole lifestyle. He wanted to be that writer, just like her. Wearing new clothes all the time and with a mind like a steel trap, storing the snippets of salty dialogue he overheard as he explored the city all that summer.

He wanted to arrive at the studios and the meetings like Liz did, swinging his bags and looking confident that he could do anything, deliver any kind of script, and be back on the doorstep with rewrites the very next day if need be. He wanted feedback and commissions and more commissions and repeat fees and parties and awards and everything that Liz was filling up his head with...

*

But then Kevin the producer and his script editor Bill called him in for a series of one-to-one meetings.

Ian left each one feeling bruised and confused.

Every draft he did of his single episode seemed to get worse and worse, in their eyes.

'Can't you see?' Kevin shouted. 'It's just *shitty*! And it's getting *shittier and shittier*! And that's why we've called you in, yet again, for an emergency meeting this time. We want to give you every chance to get it right, but that only goes up to a certain point. We're getting to the stage where my Exec needs to see this and I'm not happy about handing it over in this state. This, what you've written, Ian – five times now – is still shit. It's worse than shit. It's like the *scum* on the shit it was five drafts ago.'

Bill the script editor smiled and shrugged from behind his computer.

Ian didn't know what to say. It was like all his life force was draining out of him via the squeaky swivel chair he was sitting on. He hardly dared move or breathe.

He saw that he had got everything completely wrong.

Kevin was going on, 'We think you're good. Or, we did do, at the start. But you've lost it completely, haven't you? Look at this. Have you even read it back through? It doesn't make any sense at all. No one, not one of them, is talking about what they should be talking about. It's as if you've completely ignored the story-lining document and gone off in your own direction. What are all these twats talking about? Frigging *nonsense!*'

Ian tried to break in, saying that he was trying to show how distant the characters were from each other by giving them rather stilted chitchat…

'*Stilted chitchat?*' Kevin shouted. He was getting a bit shrieky by now. He actually stood up and for a moment Ian thought he was going to punch him. 'Who wants to listen to stilted frigging *chitchat*? Is that why we shell out millions of pounds to produce quality, ratings-grabbing, *world class* telly? Is that what our viewers want to sit down to watch? Is that why they want to vote for us at the frigging BAFTAS and the TV Quick awards? The Stilted Chitchat Show? Are you frigging *joking*? They want drama. Quality frigging *drama*. And do you know what that is, Ian?'

He was looking down at his script. Kevin was right. It was terrible. Ian must have been in a dream. What had he been thinking of? Battering away at Liz's word processor in her ground floor flat. Staring through the venetian blinds at the geese wobbling by and the cats slinking under the cars. Going over and over the same scenes and crunching down the lines of dialogue till they were as small and as real as he could make them.

'Drama isn't what you've written. Drama is her saying, 'Look, Mike. I know you don't love me anymore.' And him saying, 'I do, Hannah! I love you more than ever!' And her going, 'No, you're lying!' And him going, 'But I do!' And her saying, 'I can feel it. Deep down. I know what's true.' There! That's off the top of my head but there's more real drama in that than the pile of shite you've given us. It's pathos! It's real life! And it's eight million bastards sat at home on their settees thinking, 'Shit! She's actually saying it! She's coming out with the *truth*! The truth what's in her fucking *heart*!'

That's eight million inarticulate bastards, Ian, and they're all living dull little lives full of awkward *chitchat*. You see, they want to hear the twats on telly saying exactly what's in their heads. They want to hear those twats saying exactly what they mean. They want her to tell him he's wrong when he lies and tells her he still loves her. We all know he's talking out of his arse and we want to hear her call him out! That's *drama*, Ian. That's *soap*. That's fucking *telly*. And you haven't got a clue about it. Everything you've turned in for three months has been just frigging awful. You haven't got a clue about bringing out the subtext. It's clear you never knew what we were on about at all. And so, you've had your last chance, lovey. And you're *out*.'

      Before he knew it, Ian was out in the corridor. He caught a glimpse of Bill the script editor giving him a sympathetic look. The door slammed, and he heard even more shouting, a bit muffled.

      Then he was leaving. He was heading back to the lift. He was out of there.

      Later, as he had a few drinks with Liz at Manto's and watched the sun going down over the tall rooftops and everyone coming out to play, he basked in her commiserations. After a while he realized that, while she was sorry for him, she wasn't saying that Kevin was in any way wrong.

'I did try to tell you,' she said. 'All this all-round-the-houses dialogue you do. It's just bollocks. You've got to figure out what the story is and just tell it, in the plainest, most direct way possible. Don't over-complicate things. And don't go giving quite straightforward characters mixed feelings, whatever you do. Mixed feelings are for twats.'

By the end of that evening he was thoroughly confused and he had decided once and for all that writing was not for him. Obviously, he was hopeless. He saw the whole thing arse-about-face. He just couldn't cut through the irrelevant crap of everyday life – that's how Liz had tried to explain it. By then they were both hopelessly drunk, hugging each other clammily in the corner of the smoky New Union bar. They were completely out of their trees.

'You think you ought to be giving people... What's that shitty, old-fashioned phrase? Oh yeah. A slice of life. Well, that doesn't exist, Ian. There's no such thing. You think everyone wants realism and being true-to-life and everything left open-ended. Well, no one wants to watch that. Not on telly. We want proper endings. Happy. Sad. Weddings. Murders. Revenge. We want everything larger than life. We want it more colourful. More... aspirational. That's the word. We don't want a whole load of drongos mithering on about fuck-all...'

Ian was marveling at her: she had an amazing talent. Cutting all the crap out of life. Seeing through to the true story. Making up characters that everyone could understand and feel human feelings for. Ian longed to be like that, and to have that knack.

And, also, he longed not to have mixed feelings about anything ever again.

He had been invited to Manchester and to take on this commission as a complete fluke. Eventually they had found him out. He was a fake. And so he had been expelled.

But – under the lit-up trees and the looming glass fronts of bars, crazy with dancing shadows – he realized he was still in love with Manchester and being out on a Friday night. He loved being so pissed with Liz that he lost whole portions of his evenings and days like he'd wandered out during the ad break and not come back in time. He woke up on some floors and in some beds he couldn't remember getting into, in parts of the city he'd never explored before.

And he hardly ever went back to Sunderland after that.

And he was still in Manchester, all these years on.

*

He saw Liz again, about twelve years later. It was at a dykey bar in Chorlton, and he was there with some friends it turned out they had in common. By then Liz was a big deal in TV drama and she had a reputation for hard-hitting dramas about women or children going missing and feisty female detective inspectors. She had bought a much bigger house in West Yorkshire by now.

'Wow, look at you,' she said. 'I remember when you were all wide-eyed and innocent and wearing baggy T-shirts and your hair was all straggly. You look good, Ian.'

He shrugged and asked about her murder shows. She was charmingly self-deprecating. 'I write about people with mixed feelings now,' she laughed. 'Well, psychopaths. They have mixed feelings.'

'I thought it was just the opposite?' Ian asked. 'Out of everyone, I thought psychopaths saw things relatively simply?'

She gave him a funny look and mumbled something about her team of researchers and experts. Then she said, 'I think you got a rough ride back then, when they sacked you out of hand like that. You were trying too hard to fit in.'

'It's a long time ago. It's okay.'

'But it was going to be your career. What have you done for money since? What have you been doing with your life?'

He muttered a bit about a few of the different jobs he'd had. Bars and volunteering. How he'd tried out bookselling.

She suddenly went, 'You see, I reckon there are just two kinds of writers in this business.'

He wasn't really interested. She was being loud and fierce in a lesbian bar in Chorlton, enjoying the fact that people were noticing her and recognizing her. She was the famous writer who got on This Morning and Loose Women, talking about her shows. Ian's mates were going on about moving on, finding somewhere open for chips and he longed to go with them.

Liz was saying: 'There are hacks and there are prima donnas. I'm a prima donna.'

'No shit,' he laughed.

'And you, Ian, were trying to be a hack. But you can't blend in. You couldn't make your voice sound like just anyone else's. That's a very special talent those hacks have, and those writers who can do that will always do really well for themselves. They can make their voices sound like what their producer wants. But you can't do that. You really went about listening to real people and trying to write like they talk, didn't you?'

He nodded dumbly, feeling like a fool. He'd always listened to people. He loved listening to them.

'That wasn't what they wanted.'

'I know that now.' He sighed and watched his friends receding, disappearing out of the crammed bar. Was he the only bloke in there, now?

'You should have been doing your own kind of thing, in your own voice, or the voices of your silly, irrelevant characters that no one would care about but yourself. You should never have listened to Kevin, or Bill, or the Exec, or me, even.' She smiled. 'Even me.'

She was looking quite a bit older, Ian thought. Her skin was parched and thinner, somehow. She was giving him advice and he should be listening nicely and taking note and looking fully appreciative. People probably paid for her expertise.

He saw that she was waiting for him to be grateful. These were her pearls of wisdom. They were hard won. He probably hadn't been as shitty a writer as they'd led him to believe, back then.

'Well,' he said. 'That's interesting, I guess…'

'I used to feel so sure about everything,' Liz sighed. 'And that feeling stayed for a little while, even a few years after I last saw you. But I think a bit differently now. I think life's more complicated. I certainly think people are more complicated.' She shook her head and blinked, like she was coming out of a trance. 'Look, what are you writing now? Anything good? You could always wing it over to me, you know? You could always show it to me...'

Ian stared at her and he knew that his expression must have seemed odd. 'I'm not writing anything,' he said. 'I haven't written anything since back then. Not since you and Kevin and everyone at the studio said I was shit and wasting everyone's time.'

She laughed with embarrassment. 'What..?'

'You put me off ever wanting to write anything again.'

She looked appalled and disbelieving, then finally, miffed. 'But, if that's the case,' she said. 'You couldn't really have wanted it, could you? If you were so easily put off. It couldn't have been the thing for you. I don't believe you really wanted to be a writer at all, did you?'

He shrugged at her. It wasn't worth arguing about. Certainly it was too late to argue about now. Thinking about those script meetings just made him cringe.

'What do you do now, then?' she asked. 'I mean, *really* do. Not bar work and cafes and shit stuff. Or shops. Not for a living. I mean, what do you do with all your time?'

He remembered a conversation like this from before. He remembered her saying, ten years ago or more: 'What do people *do* all day? If they don't write or think about writing? What the hell do they think *about*?' Even at the time he'd thought that sounded unhealthy and mad.

'Actually,' he said. 'I *read*. I read proper books. That's what I grew up to be in the end. Someone who *reads*.'

All the Lady Writers of the Grange-Over-Sands Hotel Workshop

The first writing class I ever taught was in Grange-over-Sands, near the Lake District.

I had been recommended by the professor who'd been in charge of the MA I'd just finished that summer. I was living in Lancaster, at the end of a terrace of doll-sized houses by the canal. The people who ran extra-mural classes in the area were short of a tutor for a ten week course in Creative Writing in a small coastal town, some thirty miles north of Lancaster, and my professor had suggested me.

That's how I found myself catching a train one Tuesday afternoon in October, and for all the following Tuesdays till Christmas 1992.

It was a stunning journey, through small grey towns and bright forests and steep valley floors. I saw the woods turn every colour from lush, verdant green to gold and scarlet and then stark black and silvered with snow. After the forests of Silverdale the train line emerged into the flat brown sands of Morecambe Bay and the train seemed to fly across the very water itself towards the headland and the distant, toy-like town of Grange-over-Sands.

The whole trip there and back each week had a touch of magic about it.

The classes were held in an Edwardian hotel, not far from the station. It took me about two hours getting there, door to door. There was an epic quality about my Tuesday afternoons – not least for the glimpse of Cumbrian mountains in the distance and the grey sash of the Irish sea.

I met my class in the public lounge, in front of a tall fireplace. We sat in a circle of high-backed armchairs. As the days drew in shorter, and colder, the fire would be lit for us and we'd sit together with the flames flapping and crackling and shadows dancing round the room as freezing rain blew against the hotel windows. It felt like we were there to tell grand, heroic stories aloud, sharing them round the campfire.

Halfway through our two hour session each week a waitress would bring in a golden hostess trolley, tinkling with china cups and saucers and weighed down by plates of chocolate biscuits and cream cakes. The ladies of the Grange-over-Sands writing class would put down their books and pens at once and fuss about over the trolley in their haste over who would be mother this week.

They were all, of course, ladies. And they were all over retirement age.

In the first week I gathered that their usual tutor – who had moved on to do something else, but who had worked with them for quite a few years – had been female and closer to their own average age. They looked at me indulgently, that first day I turned up. Twenty-two and male and, I think, probably quite shy-seeming.

The first thing I had to learn – and learn fast – was to talk more loudly. My twelve elderly ladies were all rather deaf.

'What? Speak louder, young man! What? What's he saying? Is he talking?'

This went on for the first half of my first afternoon, as I tried to outline who I was, and what I thought I'd be doing with them in this new class of ours. I had all sorts of ideas I'd like to share with them for how our time together was going to work. Ideas which…

'Is he still talking? I can't hear a word! Can you tell what he's saying?'

I was scalding red with shame. I sat there with my new cardboard folders and class lists and notebooks. I sat there clutching my notes about how I thought we might organize ourselves. And already I was dying on my feet. I dried up. I coughed a bit. Now they were all talking and rustling amongst themselves, turning to each other and complaining loudly about how they couldn't follow me. And I heard something about what a lovely, clear speaking voice 'Marion' had had. Marion had been my predecessor.

One of the younger women was sitting closest to me, and she took pity. 'You must raise your voice and speak more slowly,' she said, kindly. 'You must think about our poor, deaf old ears and slow wits.'

I nodded, smiling and looked down at my notes. I'd filled pages and pages of A4 with thoughtful scribbles, just the day before. I'd rattled through them all in my first ten minutes, and no one had followed a single word, it seemed. All this stuff about Magical Realism and the Postmodern Novel and vernacular story-telling. All this nonsense.

What had I been thinking of? It seemed so pretentious and silly. Completely unsuitable for this class. Useless! Stuff that had been in my head. Stuff that interested me. Stuff that fired me up. Franz Kafka, Gabriel Garcia Marquez, Angela Carter, Angus Wilson. But why was I so sure that these women wanted to hear about all of this? What had any of it got to do with their afternoon writing class?

I had been trying to introduce myself and what I was all about.

And I hadn't even been able to talk loudly enough for them to hear.

Such a fool. Why should they give a toss about my magical realism and my writing about the council estate I grew up on? Did I really think they'd be bothered about what I thought about the State of the Novel Today?

'I think,' said the nice lady to my left. 'You'd better speak up. Or you may have a full-scale riot on your hands pretty soon. These old dears can become rather fierce, you know.'

I nodded. I cleared my throat.

Speaking too softly and quietly had been the bane of my life up till now. I gabbled, too, running one word into the next, as if my thoughts were moving faster than my mouth could. I leapt from thought to thought and idea to idea. That might be okay in a student, but it was hopeless in someone trying to teach. I had to make myself plain.

This wasn't about me expressing my thoughts and ideas.

It was about *them*. The ladies of Grange-over-Sands.

In a flash I realized that I didn't have to do as much talking as I thought. I was just gabbling away to fill up the ominous silence, wasn't I? I was actually rather scared of them and the ornate public room and the very thought of my callow, over-complicated words echoing around it. I was talking quieter so I wouldn't feel such a fool.

But that was no good. I had to be bolder and braver than that.

I tucked my notes about myself and my own thoughts on fiction writing away, into my new cardboard folder. 'Well, that's enough about me,' I said in a voice almost completely new to me. It was definitely louder and bolder. 'What about you lot?'

They stopped muttering to each other and rustling and fiddling with hearing aid dials. They turned to me, some of them smiling.

'That's better,' someone said.

'Has he started talking now?' said another.

They were all dressed up for their afternoon out. I could see that now. Ruffly blouses and woollen two-pieces. Even a bit of jewellery in evidence. Some were more casually dressed. But they were all sitting there with notebooks and pens at the ready. They were keen. This was their afternoon out, having a class. This was where they came to express themselves. To write stories and bits of memories. To put things down in pen and ink. They knew how these classes ought to work. They'd been doing it for years.

And now they were relieved that I was talking properly and I was suggesting an exercise where they wrote and talked all about their lives, by way of introducing themselves to me.

I also saw that they were as nervous of me as I was of them. For all their bluster and moaning aloud about losing their beloved Marion, they were anxious about whether this was going to work out. But they wanted it to. We all wanted it to. We wanted to have a series of lovely autumn afternoons together, learning something.

Just then, with a bit of kerfuffle, in came the oldest lady of the lot, some forty minutes late. She was bent almost double with a dowager's hump, and wore a tweed cape rather raffishly. She came shuffling in with the aid of a stick, moving heavily between the high-backed chairs of the lounge until she reached us. A space was cleared deferentially. Evidently she had high status among the ladies of Grange-over-Sands. She stared at me beadily, and started messing on with her hearing aid. It whined and she frowned and fiddled with it.

My next door neighbour glanced at me and smiled encouragingly. I must have looked very scared indeed.

Then the new arrival looked straight at me and beamed. 'Come along then, young fella. I hope you're going to impress us. We're in your expert hands. What do you want us to do?'

'Okay,' I said, very loudly. 'Shall we begin?'

ınion Piece

Already it had been one of those daft weeks, when things are going wrong and they pile up so thickly that all you can do is laugh. I'd lost my wallet containing all my vital cards on Tuesday, somewhere between the back of a taxi and my own front door. It wasn't till the next day I realised and hunted the house alone, panic-stricken. I rushed outside and hunted there as well, staring at the gutter and under the neatly trimmed hedges. It was a week in which I could take this to be a symptom of stress.

    I had imagined myself on top of things. It was everyone else who was inept and busily messing things up on my behalf. I waited indoors to receive a registered parcel and it took thirty-seven hours to arrive because the Royal Mail couldn't find my house. That very week I was meant to be changing publisher, but the vital meeting in London couldn't happen because my old publisher hadn't faxed the relevant shit sales figures to the new lot. My bank was having a wonderful time sending me, the solicitor, and their own Birmingham superiors, all the wrong paperwork concerning my mortgage. My mortgage advisor explained it thus: 'Someone has pressed the wrong button again!'

And so any lapse on my part I was bound to take as a symptom of stress.

I was sad to lose the wallet, mostly because it was a replacement my mam had sent me, three years before, with a tenner pushed inside, when my last one was stolen on campus.

Stupidly, I had left a blank cheque inside, just in case of emergencies. I could picture it: rubbed thin as onion paper, but still potently useful and I couldn't for the life of me remember the number in order to put a stop to it. I've never balanced a cheque book in my life. I phoned my bank and made stabbing guesses at the number based on blank stubs and my recent history showing on the bank teller's VDU in Edinburgh: 177, 179, 176. And all I could think about was someone fishing the wallet out of the gutter outside my house, rushing off and cleaning the account out before I even got a chance to pay the hefty deposit on my house.

So it was in the middle of this that I had to meet one of my icons.

Norwich had been hot for a fortnight. It was May and we seemed to get the sort of shimmering, standing, gelid heat you'd imagine on the Broads, across miles of empty fens. Norwich was green and musty-smelling and just the night before, the Saturday night, the heavens had opened for a brief half hour after first dark, landing the fattest, wettest rain drops I could remember. I dashed outside to walk in it as long as it lasted, my face up to the sky, breathing in the ozone and the smell of the rain sluicing dust off everything.

Sunday morning it was hot and bright all over again. I jotted down some questions at the kitchen table, gulping coffee and smoking. I always get nervous as hell doing these appearances and talking in front of an audience, though I seem to do it quite a lot.

What's your best memory of being on television?
What made you leave the show after so long?
How much of Debs were you allowed to invent?
What do you think Debs is doing now?
Who chose your outfits?
Is it true that you wrote your final scene?

What made me slightly anxious about the audience thing this time was that, also that week, I had got myself my very first serious stalker. She had come to a public reading I gave the previous month and sent me anonymous and, at first, rather flattering and overwritten letters, all about snails and leopards and hunting through the undergrowth of the collective psyche. Then suddenly one morning in my office I clicked up my new emails and discovered a note in which she asked whether or not I was scared about the multiplicity of versions of me I'd generated with my 'depressingly beautiful' stories and how she wanted to own them all for me. 'I wish I could kill you,' she typed, 'but I can't, and doesn't that make you terribly afraid?'

Jesus, I thought, and laughed. Then I told some others, who came to my office to drink coffee and smoke at the usual time and they made me think I should be concerned. I realised how exposed I was in my office, with students passing by all day long and knocking on the door and coming in, to tell me all sorts of stuff. They usually felt quite easy about breezing in and saying, 'Oh, are you writing? What are you writing?' Almost a year into my teaching job and most people there knew me and they came in all the time to chat and have a look. What if, some day, a woman I never recognised came in and started on about snails and leopards and the Death of the Author? No more staying back after hours, I decided.

Anyway, the audience I was getting up in front of this Sunday was quite different. Not students, not literature freaks, not Cult Studs. They were science fiction fans. A quite different kettle of queer fish.

I walked into town with my questions and got to the shop too early. I sat in the cafe across the road, on a squashy blue sofa in their window and wrote a whole tiny scene for my new novel, which was progressing nicely and chronologically. The cafe had just opened and the staff were still clustered at the counter, chatting and surprised to see someone coming in so soon. The manager was saying to his young waitress, 'Oh, god; to be eighteen and beautiful again.'

When I stopped writing and had my coffee, asking specially for the little bowl of cocktail sugar I knew they had there, I felt like I was going off to the gallows. I don't know why I say I'll do these things. These events. They always involve meeting someone - usually a writer - an icon from my personal pantheon, and every time it's touch and go whether they'll go up or down in my already very sensitive estimation. Really, you shouldn't meet anyone from your pantheon. At the same time I knew why I was doing it: this abiding sense that, actually, I'll get on with the people whose work I love and we'll hit it off immediately and manage - in all the busyness - to have the Significant Talk. We'll connect and I'll be happy. But usually these people are writers and so there's always stuff to have the Significant Talk about (each other's books, publishers, publicity, reviews, business, and how you can swap tenses and persons in media res and it's like changing gears in a car, etc etc) but today was different, because Susie Gillian was an actress.

I looked at the shop across the road. They had a picture of her blown up in the window. Her face was taller than I was. She was resting her chin on one hand and gazing straight at me. A heart shaped face with dewy eyes, framed in masses of dark hair.

The sign read: 'Today at one thirty and three o'clock, Susie Gillian from TV's 'Iris Wildthyme' will answer YOUR questions and sign YOUR merchandise.' All around the poster was a mass of shiny stuff: books, rolled posters, toy figures. It was twenty years since Susie Gillian had left the cult show, but her role as Iris Wildthyme's travelling companion Debs was remembered fondly by the fans and, as it happens, by me. My blissful soaking in last night's rain had come about because I went to the video shop to rent my favourite tape, 'Iris Wildthyme and the Claws of Daemnos.' If this huge picture in the window was recent, then Susie Gillian had hardly aged at all since leaving the show. She must be fifty by now. Twenty years since she had made Iris take her back home to earth and the grouchy old woman had steered her time and space travelling double decker bus back to South London and let her beloved companion Debs out of the hydraulic doors in a quiet, suburban cul-de-sac. And Debs had wandered out of all our lives.

She came back once, in the middle of the 1980's, for the special TV movie, 'The End of Iris', in which all the companions and extravagant villains and monsters returned for one long and special romp: a big blow out which ended the gloriously outdated series for good. So it was over ten years since the series had finished and the fans still clamoured for more. It was an industry. Bella Fitzgerald, the short and dumpy and campily bad actress who had played Iris died soon after her show was cancelled. It had destroyed her, some said, the BBC pulling the plug on the role she had played for twenty five years. The fans still campaigned for the show to come back. The Americans had, in recent years, bought up the rights and made a single pilot episode of a new version, with a silicon-implanted, bleached haired foxy lady playing the reborn Iris, still schlepping about in her double decker bus, but it hadn't worked out. The show was too English, everyone said. The Americans just didn't get its irony. They couldn't get that kind of camp.

      All that kept it going was a series of novels that the BBC were producing on a monthly basis. This was a new development. In the last year they had begun a range of glossy paperbacks, each called 'Iris Wildthyme and ...' Promptly I had got myself signed up to write one and now it had been published. 'The Blue Angel' was my present to myself: a kind of writing holiday, for which I wasn't paid much, but it was fun to do and I was adding to the Iris Wildthyme mythos. And what was more, I'd included Susie

Gillian's character, Debs in the story - older and wiser - and that was the reason the bookstore people had asked me to come and meet Susie Gillian, to sign some books and interview her on the platform.

So that was the background. I felt queasy and sick. I watched one of the bookstore owners come out of his shop - a tubby fella in a goatee beard and a short-sleeved silk shirt - and dash to his car. He was off, I thought miserably, to fetch Susie Gillian from the railway station. It was almost time.

*

They'd done the inside of the shop nicely. 'I was here till eleven last night sorting out this lot,' said Daniel, the owner, who walked me through to the back. The shop was filled with rows of seats, facing two high stools, which stood either side of a set of steps before a red curtain. On my side there was a display of all my books, the novels as well as the Iris Wildthyme book. On the other side there was another vast, blown up picture of Susie Gillian. We both had glasses of water set out ready. 'She's here,' he said. 'She's in the back, titivating her hair and make up.'

As we went through the curtain to the staff room, there were already punters coming into the shop behind us. I didn't like the look of those high stools. I was sure to drop off mine. I had hoped we'd be sitting on a sofa.

She was in a chic white suit, leaning into the staff room mirror and doing her lipstick fresh when I walked in. Her hair was just as it had been in the show, twenty years before. When Daniel said, 'Ms Gillian, this is Paul, who'll be interviewing you today,' her eyes flicked across and looked at my reflection. She was leaning across a tableful of sandwiches on silver plates, carefully holding her white jacket away from them. She whirled around and smiled, offering me her hand.

'Oh, I am so glad you're here to get up on the stand with me. Usually, you get left to fend for yourself, and that's all right, but it is better with company. Do you have a light, Stephen, because I don't. I don't often smoke. Only when I'm working. My daughter never sees me smoking at all, she doesn't know I do.'

'It's lovely to meet you,' I said, and produced a lighter as she fetched out a very low tar cigarette. I thought: She called me Stephen, for some reason. Daniel, the owner, was looking on with a kind of avuncular gleam in his eye, glad he had brought us together. I remembered how he'd told me he'd met her before and she was 'a typical actress. Extremely small with a head that seems rather large. And she calls you darling and she's phoned me every day for a week and then she faxed me a photo of her thirteen year old daughter.'

I wondered what she would think about arriving in the shop and realising that all the staff were gay and that the shop's stock was given over to gay magazines and books and what you might call the paraphernalia of camp, as much as it was to science fiction and horror. Perhaps she was used to it. I'd always assumed that all fans and hangers-on of 'Iris Wildthyme' were queer.

'I like that,' Susie said, pointing suddenly to an acid coloured poster of dykes dressed as cowboys and dancing round. 'What's that?'

'A lesbian line-dancing club,' said Daniel, rolling his eyes. 'In Norwich.'

'Oh, that's very good,' she said. 'Tell me, Stephen...'

'Paul,' I said, politely.

'Oh, god. Have you come all the way from London, too? Liverpool Street was horrible.'

'I live here. I teach at the university.'

'How clever of you!'

'But I was at Liverpool Street two weeks ago at midnight, waiting for the last train and it was awful and full of football fans shouting that they were going to Wembley.' I had kept my head down and carried on reading a biography of WH Auden.

In the small space of the staff room I realised I'd put too much Davidoff on. Susie smelled of moisturiser, I thought, something that kept her skin glowing like that. She looked incredible for fifty.

'You don't look old enough to teach,' she said. 'That's what I think.'

I was twenty-eight. At that age, Susie Gillian was about to leave the series after three years in the supporting role. She'd left when I was seven, the year that my parents divorced. I couldn't tell her that, though. That one of my earliest memories was of her face on our telly, screaming blue murder in fright.

Daniel had popped out the front again. He came back and asked us to stand ready by the curtain. 'We're full up,' he said. 'They're all in their seats.' We could hear them chattering loudly. I had a quick look through the gap. They were mostly in their thirties, all clutching books and magazines and odd-looking dolls and figurines. On the front row was a small middle-aged woman dressed as Iris Wildthyme, and a child, the only child in the place, in a football outfit.

Daniel said he'd do our introductions and he would announce me as a bonus guest. He said he was nervous now and

Susie shushed him. She thought he meant stage fright, but I think he meant that the shop had to shift eight hundred pounds' worth of merchandise to break even today. He went out and there were murmurs all the way through his little talk.

'What do I call you?'

'Call me Susie.'

She was psyching herself up. She smiled broadly and it stayed. 'Tell me I haven't got anything in my teeth.'

I thought how odd it was. The two of us stranded behind the curtain and everyone else out front. It all seemed to be up to me, suddenly.

'I do hope they've kept their word and not sold a ticket to Billy Shane,' she said.

'Who's that?'

'He writes to me every single day. I stopped replying three years ago, but it doesn't deter him. He sometimes tries to get into my events, but I won't have him.'

Then, when she heard her name, Susie Gillian pulled back the curtain and stepped quickly down the steps to gasps and applause. I followed and watched where I was stepping.

'How nice of you all to come,' she said, and I was feeling my way carefully onto the wobbling high stool. Between us was the robot cat thing the shop had borrowed from the BBC. In the show, the robot cat thing had been Debs' futuristic pet. Today it was an added draw. It was a horrible, tatty, unrealistic looking thing. Daniel was scared in case it got trashed. I thought it was funny that Susie hadn't mentioned its being there, but I was disappointed, too, as if the fact of her not acknowledging the cat thing spoiled the illusion for me. Beside the cat thing there was a tin, filled with strips of paper. The audience had written out questions they wanted Susie to answer. I rattled them around and plunged in. But I wanted to ask my own as well.

*

We did forty minutes of chat. She was very kind and answered at length. She sat with her hands on her thighs like a Principal Boy and projected and very expertly told her behind-the-scenes stories of the show. What it was like to have a giant lobster stuck with velcro to your back. The pranks that cast and crew would get up to. The audience - many of them, I realised - dressed up in characters, were rather boisterous. They kept shoving in with further questions of their own.

    I asked my question about how the subtext of the series was really about Iris and Debs being in love.

'She loved her, didn't she?' I said, and there were gasps. 'And she loved her?'

Susie looked perplexed. 'There was no sexy stuff aboard the magic double decker bus!' she cried, and everyone laughed.

*

We had to sit in the window signing things. Embarrassingly, the staff had set out a place for me right beside Susie and, as the queue shuffled up, I assumed they would be after her and not me. I was still embarrassed from a reading I gave in Glasgow that January, when I read with a much more established 'gay writer' and we were jampacked in a little corner for 'gay books'. On that occasion it reminded me of school, how we had to gather on the story rug, at Mrs Payne's feet, ready for story hour. In Glasgow I was mortified by the large and rather bullish events organiser who made up for the audience's relative quiet by asking stupid questions (he asked me, because I wrote about women and working class women at that, did that make my fiction less literary and more like something off the telly?) Anyway, when the readings were done and the punters shuffled up (what a mixed bunch we had) that events organiser came up with a vast pile of hardbacked stock for my fellow reader to sign. He didn't bring mine. He assumed, evidently, that he could happily send them back to whichever warehouse they'd come from. My fellow reader was affably subversive, once the organiser's massive back was turned. He gave me his fountain pen and told me to sign everything in sight. 'It's how we make our living. So they can't send any of the bastard things back.' On the window sill of Gay Corner we signed everything: even each other's, and we even signed some as Barbara Taylor Bradford.

 I knew a woman poet in the North who laughingly said her hobby was 'collecting detritus from famous poets.' In a glass vial she had a shred of dandruff from the bowed head of Stephen Spender. It had dropped into her opened volume as he signed it for her. She slammed the book shut, pressing it and later tweezed it out at home. It was a joke, she said, but I thought: she still kept it. Like those test tubes you can buy, supposedly containing a dribble of Elvis sweat, or a wart.

 So people brought me things to sign, as Susie and I sat at the table, which was laid with a cloth of fake leopard skin. They got me to sign my book as they waited for her. She made sure she talked to everyone, very loudly, and asked them questions. Some she vaguely remembered from other events, and the presents they had given her then. 'Remind me, though, because I'm terrible with names.'

One man - though he didn't look happy about it - had bought two of my non-Iris Wildthyme novels. 'Because I'm a completist,' he said. His beard was bristling and black and all the buttons down his paisley shirt looked tight over his belly.

They were buying video tapes of episodes of the show, pulling the covers out from under the laminate, and Susie was signing the inner spine. I thought, they won't be able to read that anyway. I'd never heard of people signing video tapes before.

'I'm signing things,' she said, 'though I don't know if I even get a penny from them. Still, it's part of the job and it spreads the good word.' As she talked to me, she still directed the words at the now rather subdued punters. This close up they were quieter. They didn't care what she was saying. Suddenly Susie's voice hardened and she flashed her eyes at me. 'I do think there are a lot of rip-off merchants out there. Selling pictures and tapes and stills of me and I don't get a penny! I don't even own my face! I'm taking legal action, actually, did I tell you? I'm going to the union about this. I'm doing it for the sake of all actors. The Beeb don't care. And now there's no TV show they don't know anything about it. But as I see it, they have an obligation to see that we don't get ripped off. Look at this!' She waved a six inch high doll of herself at me. 'Who's making these? Where does all the money go? Someone's pockets.' She looked at the doll. It had steel bolts in its elbows and knees. 'It looks nothing like me,' she said thoughtfully. 'But it's clearly intended to **be** me. And that's a liberty.' Then she sighed and said, sotto voce, 'Don't you find the fans very demanding?'

I said I did. In Glasgow, when I did my reading, which had nothing to do with science fiction, I still had Iris Wildthyme fans in the audience. They knew my name from the news page of the Iris Wildthyme magazine. They didn't make themselves known until the end when one of them, a pretty, girlish student with long dark hair over his face came up and asked, did I have any teasers for what 'The Blue Angel' was going to be about? At that point, I barely knew myself. I would sit down with a bottle of gin in February and make up four hundred pages of mad stuff. I told him I was rewriting the Arabian Nights Entertainments backwards, and my book would feature Queens in huge jars of scarlet jam, golden bears who shaved off their fur, alligator men and wish-granting djinn.

'You can't tell them to bugger off, though,' Susie said. 'Not when they're your bread and butter.'

I told her the story that the editor of the new Iris Wildthyme books had told me. He was at an event in a pub, in honour of the new books, and the Iris Wildthyme fans came out en masse. They were more interested in when he would organise the reissuing of the videos of the old episodes. The fans couldn't get their hands on their favourite old stories. Especially, I told Susie, the classic in which Susie left the show. She was very flattered about this.

'Anyway,' I said. 'When Simon, the editor, went to the lav, thinking he'd escaped them for a minute, he was at the urinal and there was someone shuffling up beside him. Oh help, he thought. Then this rather querulous voice asks him, 'So tell me, when are you going to put out 'The Hand of Terror'?'

I laughed and Susie nodded. 'That's exactly what they're like.'

Then someone wanted a photo and Daniel the bookstore owner was coming through the crowd, lugging the horrid mechanical cat thing. People wanted their photo with it and Susie together.

I took my cue (I had this odd aversion to the lifeless metal thing) and went to the staff room again, to see what wine they had on the go. They'd promised some.

Daniel had made some crack about me not being able to get up in front of a crowd without a couple of drinks inside me. Too bloody right.

*

In the staff room the staff were eating the sandwiches and cakes. One of the boys from the till had made them and they were stuffed with roast peppers and brie and grapes. A younger member was saying, 'Whoever puts grapes in sandwiches?'

'I do,' said a butch girl in leather. It turned out she came from an official Iris Wildthyme fanzine. 'I put peach with ham, grapes with chicken, and apricots with … anything I like.'

They boy pulled a face. He had a model of the double decker bus from the show that he'd bought from stock and he wanted Susie to sign the card. He was fanning himself with it. The boy responsible for the sandwiches gave me a glass of white wine. It was very hot in the windowless staff room. Daniel's partner, who was older and bigger, came in with his middle-aged sister in tow. He laughed when they told him the boy with the bus was too shy to get his merchandise signed. 'You can't be shy. You've got to make her sign the whole bloody shop, everything in it, before she leaves tonight.' He gave me an odd smile. 'This is my sister, Emily. She missed all your questions. She's just arrived. She doesn't like Iris Wildthyme at all.'

She was very small, in a pink blouse. She was wearing Rose West glasses. 'Did you never want to be an actor?' she asked. 'On the other side of the silver screen, like her out there?'

'I'm a writer,' I said, and realised I didn't know which side of the screen that put me on.

Susie came in. She shut the door quickly. There wasn't a seat free. 'Oh, wine,' she said happily, and Bob, the co-owner, fetched her a glass.

'That went all right, didn't it, Stephen? Paul?' she smiled. 'I think we gave them good chat.'

'When are the next lot coming in?' I asked.

'Three o'clock,' said Bob. 'Ten minutes.'

For a second I saw Susie's face fall. She'd thought it was finished with. When people were leaving with their signed merchandise, she'd been calling out, 'Oh, going already? Don't go without saying goodbye!' With the assurance of someone whose audience is being sent happily on their way.

Daniel appeared, flustered and hot. 'They're coming in already. That trampy bloke is still there. Standing at the back. He's bought two tickets. Doesn't say a thing. Only answers to the name of Iris. He doesn't want to meet Ms Gillian, or have anything signed. He just wants to see her.'

Susie shrugged carelessly and went to the buffet. 'Ooh, sandwiches.' There weren't that many left.

'He's harmless, though,' said Bob. Everyone looked at him.

'He was stood outside the shop first thing,' said the shy salesboy. 'Waiting by the wall. I don't call that harmless.'

'I think,' said Susie suddenly, 'that it's the kind of TV show that attracts people who ... need to escape into something.'

'Sad people,' said the butch fanzine girl, with enough irony to let us know she included herself.

'But they all seem so happy!' Susie said. 'Why's that sad?'

I thought about the two men who came together. One had a twisted spine and moved along slowly with half steps. His friend was shaking and couldn't keep his gaze straight. They helped each other along in the signing line, bringing their videos, then they helped each other out of the shop again. I thought about how Susie recognised them from a do in Manchester and spoke so nicely to them, though they couldn't get the words out in reply. And there was the girl who was stuttering so badly Susie asked and checked she was okay. The girl held onto Susie's hand and said at last that she dressed like Susie's character Debs all the time, and that she made her own clothes.

'It gives me a warm feeling,' said Susie. 'It was just a silly TV programme. But it makes people happy. Look at that lot out there.'

'Five more minutes,' Bob said, and left the room with his polaroid camera at the ready. He was charging three pounds for pictures with Ms Gillian. Susie leaned for her glass and whispered to me, 'Some break this is. You can't move for people.'

'Here,' I said, 'sit here.' There was a fuschia inflatable chair by the sink. She sank into it, careful with her red wine and white suit.

'Hey, Colin,' said Daniel. 'You said you'd do your re-enactment when she was here.'

Daniel was being a bit raucous, I thought. He was the one who had instructed his staff to call her Ms Gillian and to treat her like Joan Crawford for a day. Now he was red in the face and sipping wine rapidly. He said, turning to our corner, 'Colin had this whole impersonation worked out.'

'Oh, yes?' Susie asked cautiously.

'We were watching 'The Creature From Winterthorn' on video in the shop. And there's this fabulous scene where you get chased and twist your ankle and succumb to the devil.'

'I remember that,' Susie said. 'I...'

'And Colin can take you off perfectly.'

Susie braced herself. 'Let's see it, then. Come on, Colin.'

Colin was the boy who had made the sandwiches. He was laughing and weeping in the kitchen by now. He couldn't bear to come out, he said.

'Yeah, come on, Colin,' laughed Daniel. The other staff members were laughing, too.

'Colin,' said Susie. 'You have to do it, now.' She was wary, I thought, of being sent up too much.

'I can't...' he laughed. Then he came out abruptly and did a little trip and clutched his ankle. His orange trainers had three inch platforms.

Susie made sure she laughed as loudly as everybody else.

'But I've always had extremely weak ankles!' she protested. 'It was **true**!'

*

We did our second turn then. It was faster. We had been warned. We had to stop early to make sure enough gear was sold. I asked Susie if she had kept any of the outfits she wore in the show.

'Oh, in the attic,' she said. 'I've got the stripey dress from my last story. I've got some yellow moon boots. And I've got a rubber lobster. But no scripts. No pictures. I didn't think. I threw away everything. At the time, it's just another show. Now people spend a fortune on these things. A few other things I had - earrings, ray guns, souvenirs - I gave away to be auctioned in the big conventions in the US, for charity. So really, I've got very little.'

In this session, every time she came out with an insider's fact, some tidbit of gossip, a man in the third row couldn't help barking out, 'I know, I know, I already know that.' Susie was starting to blush and flag.

At the signing table she asked me about my own novels. I asked Daniel - who was taking the hideous cat thing away again - to pass me a copy of my latest, 'As If By Magic.' He came back with it, pushing through the crowd. 'Make sure you tell Bob you've got it,' he said, with a nod. Perhaps, I thought, he means me to pay for it.

'This is a present,' I told her. And signed it quickly. She stowed it in her bag. Loot. Profuse thank you's and then a squawk of fright, so familiar from the show.

'Bugger! I'm so stupid. I forgot about them.' She fished out a sheaf of glossy eight by tens. 'See what I'm like? No wonder I've got no money. I forgot all about these bloody things.' She laid the pictures - publicity shots - out on the leopard skin tablecloth. 'These are three pounds, the colour are four pounds, and the postcards are two. I'll sign them all in silver.' She took out and shook a silver glitter pen. The remaining punters were roused and started to snatch the pictures up. The air riffled with the noise of glossy prints.

'I might as well get in on the act,' she said to me. 'I'm setting up in business.' Then she sighed. 'About your question, though. About keeping things. I wish I'd thought on. And kept everything. The attic could be full of valuable things. Valuable to someone, anyway. I knew at the time it was a big TV show. That it would have fans like this in the future. I say that you can't tell the future, but really you can.'

'Yeah?'

She nodded. 'In your heart, you know when the high point in your career is. You know when your glory years are. I knew mine. I knew when they were happening. But I hardly kept a thing.'

Now Daniel came over, bringing a dump-bin full of six inch figures on cards for her to sign. There was about fifty of them in there. He gave her a fresh pen.

*

I left before she did. I had a headache with wine and the heat. Soon she was going back to the station. I said she must get a taxi and avoid the football fans.

'That'll cost a fortune,' she said. 'I'll read you on the train. It looks ... different, your book.'

'Oh, it's certainly that.'

We hugged and had a polaroid taken just like that. On the white card beneath, as it developed, she wrote her love and 'Here's to the book!' in indelible marker.

'We never got time for a proper sit-down chat,' she said.

We said goodbye and that we'd talk again. Someone came in with flowers. Someone else broke the ears off the robot cat.

I walked home through the intricate streets of town.

At home I switched on everything. The video played the last thing I'd been watching. A pirate copy of 'The Hand of Terror.' The answerphone played messages. I put the stereo on and, kneeling for the plug on the electronic air freshener that took away the smell of fags, I found myself looking at a few framed post cards I'd absentmindedly hung on the wall. The cover of my first novel framed, the cover of 'BritLit Four', which was the first anthology that printed a story of mine. I was thinking about framing the polaroid of me with Susie.

When I'd put these post cards on the wall I thought maybe it was a bit pathetic. Like the cards were saying, Look what I've done!

That afternoon I thought, fuck it. This is evidence. Whatever else they are, these are my glory years. And I'm keeping everything. Every scrap of stuff that comes my way.

And, headachey, I went upstairs for a lie down. Kicking off my shoes, I knocked aside the ruffles of blue muslin that hung down as curtains in the bedroom window. Tangled in the carefully disarrayed fabric was my wallet. Cards intact. Blank cheque safely inside.

I lay on the unmade bed and laughed.

Downstairs Cilla Black sang the wonderful songs she used to sing before she changed her career to something dreadful, and the phone played back my afternoon's freight of messages.

Sit Down Next to Me

It wasn't that he felt stuck with the blind girl, exactly.

Yes, it was. He *did* feel like he was stuck with her.

Julie was so keen to be friends right from the very start, he couldn't brush her off. He couldn't be so cruel.

It all started with the Children in Need pyjama pub crawl at the end of the first term. It was the kind of thing that sounded like it would be a good laugh, and they'd be doing something worthwhile for charity.

David and his little gang met in their college bar and the six of them were dressed in pyjamas and dressing gowns and slippers. They didn't stand out too much in a bar where everyone was dressed as something or other, all keen to have fun for a charitable cause.

The bars on campus were still offering Green Bastards, which was a craze that had started at Hallowe'en and been around for a month now. Lager, cider, blue curacao. The resultant concoction was the dark green of fake Christmas trees.

Liz introduced him to a friend from her English Literature seminar group. Apparently all her friends were richer than she was and they went away every weekend. They left Julie on her own in her house block, feeling a bit left out. Liz had decided she needed befriending and bringing in.

David thought this was nice, and typical Liz. She was brash and friendly, and would talk to anyone. It was one of the things he really liked about her. Back on his first, nervy day on campus, Liz had been chatty and larger than life, down in that bleak common room and she had made him feel much better about being there. Now she was doing the same thing with Julie. Bossing her about, but in a nice way. Telling her that they were all using their dressing gown cords to tie each other's ankles together. It was all part of the daft fun of it. They'd be walking along, five abreast, down the walkways of campus, across the college quads, and into each of the bars. It would be like being in a ten-legged race.

It was just as Liz was lashing Julie's ankle to David's that he realized that the girl new in their gang was blind. That's why Liz was doing the tying for her.

Julie stood there in Marks and Spencers pyjamas, in the middle of the crowded bar, smiling at the ceiling. She looked somehow serene and excited at the same time.

Liz straightened up. 'There you are. In bondage, Julie! What do you think about that?'

Julie bent closer to hear and laughed out loud, nodding. 'Oh, yes! Funny!'

Liz clapped her on the shoulder. 'Our David will look after you. Don't you worry. He's a good lad.'

David raised his voice so it was as loud as Liz's and shouted in Julie's smiling face. 'Yes, don't worry about anything, Julie!' He wasn't sure why he'd said that. Julie didn't look in the least bit worried. She seemed – if anything – keen to place herself at the mercy of pyjama-clad pub-crawlers.

'I'll be at the other end of the line,' Liz said, and wriggled off through the crowded space. She'd already said she had to be at one end, because being tied by two ankles could bring on a panic attack.

'Do you do this a lot?' Julie shouted into mid-air and it took David a few seconds to realise she was talking to him. 'Go out, I mean? To the bars?'

He leant in close and realized that her breath smelled of some kind of sweets. Refreshers, maybe. She was a chunky girl, with short hair brushed in an odd, sticky-up style. It was disconcerting at first, when he talked to her, to see that her eyes were pointing in the wrong direction. Though, after almost a term on campus, and living with drama students, David was used to chatting away with people who looked over his shoulder, scanning everyone else in the bar.

The music was loud as ever, and the same run of songs that seemed to be on every night. Sisters of Mercy, Happy Mondays, Inspiral Carpets, James' 'Sit Down Next to Me.'

'All right, everyone,' shouted Liz, standing on a stool (the boy next to her had to lift his leg awkwardly and almost sent them all tumbling over.) 'Drink up! We'll finish these Green Bastards and move onto the Michel Foucault Lounge next. Julie – you're on the end like me. You've got to carry the other bucket.'

'What's she saying?' Julie shouted.

'The bucket. For donations!' David shouted.

'Donations for what?'

'For Children in Need! That's what we're doing this for!'

'Oh,' she said. 'Oh, yes. That's right. It's a good idea, isn't it?' She guided her pint of Green Bastard up to her mouth and started to drink the horrible stuff enthusiastically. 'Liz has some great ideas. She's such a scream. We have a real giggle in our Contemporary Novel Module. She's one of the reasons I'm still here, actually.'

David didn't have a chance to shout any more questions at her, because Liz and the others were yelling at him to get on with his Bastard so they could all move on.

*

Liz's bucket of donations got lost somewhere between the Jacques Lacan and the Simone de Beauvoir bar. There wasn't much money in it, because after the first couple of pints they had forgotten about trying to get money off anyone. It had been enough just to stay upright and keep on downing awful drinks.

Most of the campus walkways were covered and sheltered from the freezing wind and rain that were blowing over the fields that surrounded the university. Only when they crossed the paved square in the middle and wandered to the far outposts at the southern end did they get completely soaked and frozen.

When they struggled all the way to Simone De Beauvoir College it was like battling with arctic conditions and Julie started to get almost hysterical. David wasn't sure what to do. She was shouting and going a bit funny and he didn't know how to handle it. It would be awful if she died suddenly of exposure and when the ambulance men came to get the body they found a blind girl with all this green booze in her system, and her leg tied to David's by dressing gown cord.

Anyhow, they made it, and it was only much later on they discovered that Julie's bucket had gone AWOL somewhere on the crawl. They agreed that was better than what had happened to Liz's donation bucket, because she'd vomited into hers at the very end of the night and someone – not Liz – had had to wash all the money.

When David and Liz talked about these things the next day, hungover and devouring sausage sandwiches for Sunday lunch at a canal-side pub in town, they agreed that it had probably been a mistake doing the thing for charity anyway. The buckets and the donations just got in the way. Another mistake – probably - was having quite such an enthusiastic go on the bouncy castle in the dark courtyard of Andrea Dworkin College. They were still tied together, and they were all quite drunk. The castle was slowly deflating and, as they discovered, someone had obviously pissed themselves in there at an earlier point in the evening.

David was mortified because, with their gang's very first few bounces, Julie the blind girl disappeared down a cleft like a giant arse in the middle of the subsiding castle and he couldn't pull her out. When he tried to, the dressing gown cord just got tighter. None of his other friends noticed that Julie was in trouble. She was shouting and laughing and probably thought that suffocating between giant rubber arse-cheeks was just part of the crazy fun that Liz had organized for them. But David almost died of panic and shame on her behalf.

*

David and Liz spent all of Sunday afternoon in the small town, wandering along the canal towpath and then through the winding medieval streets. Hardly anything was open on a Sunday. 'But that's all right,' Liz said. 'Cause I've got bugger all left to spend till next week.'

For the past couple of weeks Liz had been coming up to the kitchen on the top floor, where David's friend and neighbour Kevin did most of the cooking. Already the whole bunch of them were talking about looking for a house together next year, when they'd be turfed out of their first year campus rooms.

They'd only been here eight weeks. Hardly time to get used to it at all. And yet at the same time these new friends seemed like people David knew better than anyone he had ever known at school. The rooms and the halls and walkways of campus seemed more familiar than anything at home. It was like being taken to a fake little town and getting brainwashed – like that old Patrick McGoohan show, The Prisoner.

All the leaves were down now, after the prettiest autumn he'd ever seen. For a few weeks everything had been blazing, and the air was all wood-smoky and delicious. They'd been on some lovely walks round the country lanes surrounding the university and up by the castle.

By four o'clock it was twilight, and the skies over the terraced houses by the hospital were purple and bruised. Liz and David took their place at the hitching post in the long queue of students waiting for lifts back to campus.

'If I close my eyes,' Liz laughed. 'I can still see you disappearing down the middle of the bouncy castle with that blind girl.'

'Don't!' he said. 'What if she'd suffocated? And what must she have thought – me bouncing on top of her? I was trapped though, with you lot rolling about on me...'

'It was a great night,' Liz grinned. She was paler than usual today, but she still seemed very enthusiastic about the night they'd had. Her hennae'd hair was up in a scarf of glittering purple stuff, and she was wearing the pink cardigan she'd worn the first day of Freshers' week, when she was the first person to talk to him.

There was a spate of cars stopping then, picking up two or three people at a time. A removal van even stopped and up went the back door, accommodating six students, who had to cling on inside. 'I'm glad we never had to get in that,' Liz said. 'My sausage bap would have made a reappearance if I'd climbed in the back of that van.'

Luckily it was just a normal, comfortable car that stopped for them. It was driven by a business-type lady in large glasses, with a smart suit hanging in her back window. She was on the way to Manchester, she said, and would be happy to drop them at campus before she got on the motorway. Liz sat up front with her. Rick Astley was on her stereo system.

The car was warm and perfumed muskily inside. It seemed very luxurious to David.

'You're taking your life in your hands, getting into cars with strangers,' said the woman as she drove them through the fringes of town.

Liz shrugged. 'No choice, love. The buses are expensive. Plus, they stop after two on a Sunday.'

'I remember,' the woman smiled. 'I was a student here myself, donkey's years ago.'

She didn't look as old as all that, David thought. Maybe in her late thirties? He was terrible at judging ages. Maybe she was about as old as his mam.

'I loved being a student here,' she said. 'Of course, nothing I learned came in useful for my career in retail management but, you know, it was good. I learned all kinds of things… about life and that.'

Liz nodded and looked out of the passenger window as they passed through a village, then rows of neat white bungalows, and then green, rolling fields. 'We're just getting used to it all. It's been marvelous so far. All the fellas on campus! All the free time!'

'Are you two boyfriend and girlfriend, then?' asked the woman from retail management.

'No...!' Liz laughed, spluttering a little. 'We're just best mates, aren't we, David?'

'What was that?' he pretended not to hear. He was feeling quite stung that she'd laughed out loud at the very idea. What was wrong with him?

The business woman laughed, tossing back her wet-look perm and glancing in her rear view mirror. 'The thing about the best mates that you meet at uni, is that you make them right at the start. Sometimes on the very first day. And you're all discombobulated, aren't you?'

Liz shrugged. 'I guess so.'

Yes! David wanted to say. He'd spent whole two months feeling discombobulated. This wet-look perm woman knew what she was talking about.

'Well,' she said, turning the car into the campus driveway, and zooming them up the hill to the roundabout at the top. 'You make friends very quickly at your age, but watch out. The friends you make now – you can get stuck with them. For twenty years in some cases. I've only just shrugged off the last of my friends I made when I was here. It's worse than having an overdraft. Anyhow, I'll pop you down here. Bye!'

And then they were clambering out at the bus stop at the edge of the main square. The blocky buildings of uni were quiet and dark. They looked at each other as the woman's car roared off towards the motorway and Manchester. Rick Astley was still going through David's head, and it felt like he and Liz were the only two souls on campus on Sunday night.

'I've got nothing to eat in my cupboard,' Liz frowned. 'I'm absolutely starving.'

'Let's go and see what the others are cooking,' he suggested.

They hurried through the concrete labyrinth and David was struck once again with how he knew his way around the whole place. It was like he'd been here for years.

'I'm sorry I laughed when she thought we were together,' Liz said. She thought he'd gone a bit quiet, almost frosty.

'That's all right.'

'I believe it's important to be upfront about these things, so there's no awkward tension or whatever. The fact is, I don't fancy you and never will.'

He laughed, pretending to be intently examining the photocopied posters on the walls either side of the walkway: disco nights, plays at the drama studio, society meetings. 'That's good, 'cos I'll never fancy you either,' he said.

'Tell you who does fancy you,' she said.

Oh god, he thought. But he wanted to know anyway. 'Who?'

'You spent the whole of last night tied to her leg.'

'Julie?!'

'She told me last night, when I was being sick and she was helping me, rubbing my back.'

'But she's blind!'

'She said you were a lovely, sensitive young man, from the way you talked to her.' They passed the launderette and their college porter's lodge, into the courtyard beyond. Their college's design was based on the plans for a 1960s Swedish prison, went the rumour, and David could believe it. Everything managed to look both streamlined and modern, and yet oppressive at the same time.

'It's hardly flattering though,' he said. 'Eight weeks here and the only person who even notices me is blummin' blind.'

Liz laughed at him. 'Take the compliment, daft lad!'

He didn't want to take the compliment. He wanted to retreat to his room and hide under his duvet and not come out till the end of term.

But the others were having pasta slop for tea. Piss-posh Rachel had brought her wok up from the girls' kitchen downstairs and Kevin was impressing everyone with his culinary skills. They had the Top Forty playing on the kitchen radio and David found he wanted to be with everyone after all.

*

He was trying to focus on work stuff. He put some time in at the library, mooching in the narrow stacks, browsing the literature aisles on the top floor. He sat at tables that looked over the university square and watched everyone drifting by, and the crowds that settled on the broad steps in the sunshine at lunchtime. He had reading lists for all nine of his modules, with secondary reading lists and all kinds of things he was supposed to do, but he always ended up with completely irrelevant books. Novels from the wrong decade; historical surveys of the wrong subjects. Books with lots of pictures in. He couldn't bring himself to queue at the Short Loan window on the ground floor, where the much-in-demand course texts were doled out for a mere hour at a time. People would get them stamped and then run to the photocopiers in the foyer. It was all a bit frantic and businesslike down there.

He spent hours in the Winnie Mandela coffee bar by the entrance of the library, where it was very smoky and the sandwiches and cakes were kept under glass bell jars. The coffee was bad, but the music was loud and the place was always full of sociology students and Socialist Workers and mature students with babies and toddlers. Occasionally hefty hardbacks would drop past the window onto the grass outside as someone in the toilets upstairs liberated them and others scurried out to fetch them like contraband.

David tried to read the stuff he was supposed to read – text books about sociolinguistics and stuff about existentialism and the Post-War novel – but he kept going back to his Pan paperback copy of Dracula for comfort reading. It was one of ten favourite books he had allowed himself to pack before coming to college. He could only bring three bags on the coach over the Pennines and so space had been at a premium. He had four shirts, two pairs of jeans, a jumper, a cardy, ten novels, a cassette-radio-alarm and a carry-case with twenty Boots C-90 cassettes, onto which he'd taped his forty favourite vinyl records. He'd made little cassette covers for them, too, with swirling water colour designs.

Dracula was falling apart, every time he picked it up to read it. All his books were coming apart with multiple readings. He liked the Spartan effect of them on his shelves. Essentially, his room was a bit like a prison cell, with bare brick walls and a lino floor. But it was painted a cheery yellow and he had a large window that looked out over fields and the M6 and a long stretch of woodlands. That autumn he loved to sit up all night and watch the dawn come up over the motorway, listening to the Cure, the Smiths and Enya.

One thing that stopped his room from being quite so much of a prison cell was all the people he packed into it each night. Somehow his room had become the lounge for most people in his house block. He didn't mind them smoking in there. He didn't smoke himself, but he loved the smell. They drank wine in paper cups and he'd put black candles bought from the Union shop in them and let them burn down into weird blobby shapes.

They'd make gallons of tea and eat toast at three in the morning, heaping each slice with marmalade or jam. Conversation was loud and raucous. It was often about their courses, as everyone grappled with the things they were supposed to be learning about ('What if there's nothing to the world apart from just language *itself*?') and there was a bit of argy-bargy, mostly between the kids who'd been to private school and those who felt strongly about political things and social awareness.

David loved being around all those raised voices and people shouting each other down as they sat in his room. It felt like the kind of thing that people were supposed to do at college. And they were unscary arguments, too. They were just about things and issues and stuff. No one was getting hurt. No one was going to get beaten up or upset.

He went to his lectures, one after the next, most of them concentrated in the first half of the week. Long days sitting in the rafters of climate-controlled rooms, listening to Swedish Phd students talking about linguistic analysis. Liz burst into tears that Tuesday because she couldn't understand a single word of the linguistics lecture. There was an emergency gathering that night in David's room so they could try to work out what it was all about, and it turned out that she was crying not just because she thought she would fail her course and get chucked out of uni, but she was involved in some kind of entanglement with a third year Law student who lived at the top of the tower that was famed for suicide. He was doing her head in. He was Liz's third boyfriend of the term and she thought she needed some single time.

'It's been a right faff on this term,' she sighed, blowing her nose on the hanky David passed her as they sat on his single bed.

'The sex has been marvelous. Really eye-opening, but I think it's about time I concentrated on my studies. My dad's been topping up my grant and he can barely afford it. He'll be furious if I get chucked out.'

David found himself blushing at the mention of marvelous sex. Again Liz was just so unashamed and unabashed about everything. He'd never heard anyone talk so frankly about rude stuff. Her being so candid had allowed him to ask a thing or two about female sexuality that he wasn't all that clear about, and she'd been only too happy to explain, and even draw diagrams on the back of his lecture notes folder.

They wandered down to the square each lunchtime. It was a special treat to go to the bakery and queue for one of their famous vegetarian pasties. Wholemeal pastry with mashed green cabbage and swede, hot with pepper and molten butter. They gobbled them down sitting on the wide steps, listening to the Chinese students protesting and the socialist workers waving their placards and the deejay from the Acid House student nightclub doing a record-scratching demonstration outside the travel agents.

'There's Belinda,' Liz nodded, as one of their housemates hurried by, trying not to show she'd noticed them. She was carrying a whole load of art supplies and had her cardy sleeves pulled down over both hands to cover the bandages. She'd tried to slash her wrists in their kitchen on Monday night with the first thing that came to hand, which was a potato peeler, and obviously not up to the job. Liz had gone with her in a taxi to A&E and quite enjoyed the excitement. Belinda had told her quite a lot about what it felt like to come live somewhere so bleak and northern, among people who were so different to yourself.

'Poor cow,' Liz sighed, blowing on her pasty. 'But she shouldn't pretend she doesn't know me, when I'm the one who helped her out. Oh! Did I tell you? I'm going to be in a play before the end of term. Someone's dropped out of 'Hamlet: Re-mixed' at the Duck Pond in Week 12 and I'm going to step in. Isn't that fantastic? It's a third year show and it's a good way of getting noticed by everyone.'

'It's great, but what about all the work you're behind on…?'

'Uh-huh,' she said, pointing at someone making their way across the square with her white stick swishing in front of her. 'Here comes your girlfriend.'

'What? She isn't…'

'Julie!' Liz was standing up and waving her arms about so that loads of people looked at her. 'Julie! We're sitting here having pasties! Come and join us!'

'I'm just off to my tap dancing class,' Julie grinned, stumbling a bit on the concrete steps. 'Hello, Liz.'

'David's here too,' said Liz, nudging him to speak up.

'David!' Julie said, and her whole face lit up as she looked the wrong way.

'Hey, have you read that strange novel for our seminar?' Liz asked. 'I couldn't get on with it at all. That woman's going to kill me if I haven't read the set text again. She's such a mardy cow. Stomach out to here, David. Wears maternity dresses and an Alice band and gets very snappy.'

'I couldn't get the book in Braille,' Liz shrugged. 'About half the set texts aren't even out in Braille. They're getting me a volunteer reader, but I can't see how that's going to work. What will they do? Follow me about all week, reciting Doris Lessing at me? How's that going to work?'

*

Julie was jaunty: that's what she was. David didn't know why it was surprising that a blind person was jaunty and funny. As they saw more of each other she seemed to become increasingly outgoing, with a quip or a funny story for every occasion. She did synchronized swimming, tap-dancing, joined Theatre Club and put her name down to do late night counseling on the phone. David – who'd joined nothing whatsoever - found that he was seeming morose and introverted when he was in her company. He had to tell himself to snap out of it.

Liz had no patience with his self-pity. 'Look, if you don't want her hanging around, just tell her. You won't hurt her feelings.'

They were at their college bar again, downing Green Bastards. Liz was gearing herself up for a date with the ghost of Hamlet's father. David, as she saw it, was just moaning. 'Of course it'll hurt her feelings,' he said. 'If I go saying we don't want you hanging round us.'

'I don't mind her,' Liz said. 'I think she's nice.'

'It's not you she fancies.'

Liz rolled her eyes. 'She just enjoys your company, daft lad. That's all.'

Julie had visited them in their house block almost every day that week. She had walked the length of campus – even on the blowiest, wettest days – tapping her stick in front of her and found them each time with unerring accuracy. She drank Green Bastards in the bar on Tuesday, putting Motown songs on the jukebox and telling David in a too-loud voice all about her childhood in south Manchester. Then she had thrashed him at table tennis in the porter's lodge. ('How?' he complained to Liz later. 'I mean, I know I've got no physical coordination and my hand-to-eye is terrible because I'm astigmatic – but she's blummin' blind! How did she beat me?'

Liz had just laughed.

Wednesday night Julie came round to David's room, having heard that this was where everyone sat up all night, talking about amazing stuff and listening to his music and drinking tea and sometimes Thunderbird wine (it was the cheapest at the Spa shop.) When she got there on Wednesday there weren't so many people as usual – and she sat looking cheery by David's desk, as if waiting for the fun to begin.

At one point – while he was telling the long, complicated story of his parents' divorce when he was seven, David mentioned that the next day he was going to be watching a Fellini marathon in the campus cinema, cramming for the timed essay on his Italian course.

'How come you're doing Italian?' Julie asked, and he had to explain the palaver at the start of the term over choosing extra Humanities subjects to fill out the modular requirements of Year One. Running between departments with paperwork, trying to get signed up, he'd felt like he was on a horrible kind of Treasure Hunt.

'You're doing Italian cinema?' she grinned. 'That's cool. I love foreign films. Could I come along?'

'Really, it's just for Italian 101 people…' he said, hating how prissy he was sounding. He thought about how empty the auditorium always was. Through the first term he had spent many Thursday afternoons sitting alone watching foreign movies. Practicing holding cigarettes and inhaling in the middle of the dark lecture theatre and loving the way the smoke went in blue spirals through the light.

Sure enough, he was in a hazy trance halfway through 'Amarcord' the next afternoon when, above the booming soundtrack and the rain drumming on the lecture hall's roof, he heard Julie clattering her way down the aisle. She was swishing her stick about and calling his name. He cringed as she said, '*Yoo hoo!*' and got shushed by the few others who were watching. He shrank in his seat, toying with the idea of pretending he wasn't there. But, next thing, she was sinking heavily into the fold-down seat beside him.

'Someone pointed you out,' she huffed in his ear. 'I said, is there a very good-looking hunky lad in here, waiting for me? Ha ha!'

'I'm nothing of the sort,' he said.

'I know. I just followed the scent of Insignia and Benson and Hedges. How's the film?'

Luckily, she kept quiet, with her ear cocked and a funny look on her face as she concentrated on the movie.

'Can you follow it?'

She nodded slowly. 'I've got some rudimentary Italian. We've been a couple of times. Venice and Florence for summer holidays. Have you been, David?'

'I've never been abroad.'

'What? Eighteen and you've not been abroad?'

'The Lake District. Norfolk to see my Nanna's family. But there was never the money to go on planes and stuff.'

'I love going abroad,' she whispered. 'In Italy and Spain and stuff, it's like I can breathe and relax and spread out somehow, you know? I think it's the heat. I always feel a bit... I don't know. *Squeezed* here at home in the cold and damp.'

He nodded. Sometimes, he had to admit, she said quite interesting stuff. And from what he'd seen in these wonderful afternoon movies, Italy looked like a fantastic, sprawling, heat-hazy place to be. People gave into their deepest feelings and expressed them loudly, and they ate big dinners at long tables out of doors.

*

The college night at the Carlton Night Club in Morecambe was the cheapest Christmas night on offer. There were other do's – Christmas balls on campus that the others were renting tuxedos for, but they were way out of his price range. And they were just for the posh kids, anyway. He'd been talked into the Carlton night out by Liz – who was still high on her triumph as Ophelia that week, even though she'd nearly drowned herself in the Duck Pond and had to be given mouth-to-mouth by Hamlet himself.

Everyone present – crouching in the dark, frosty reeds, smoking joints and passing around a bottle of absinthe – assumed the kiss of life was just part of the reimagining of the famous play. ('But it wasn't,' Liz later confided to David. 'I was a hairsbreadth from croaking. Have you ever swallowed pond water?')

And so she'd booked them in for this night out, even though everything they'd heard about it sounded horrible: how every week the free bus that went to and from Morecambe had a top deck that was running with hot vomit from all the cheap booze, and how during 'Walk Like an Egyptian' by the Bangles there'd be a competition to see how tall a pyramid each college could build by people (lads, mostly) standing on top of each other's shoulders. The winner was the one who could send someone high enough to touch the tall, gilded ceiling of the once-grand ballroom. Liz, David and others had watched agog as their college won, but the man on top fell and had his earring ripped out of his head, producing much more blood from one split lobe than you'd ever think possible.

David – who usually drank so little he was often embarrassed when it came time to buying rounds – went a bit daft that night and, after a slow start on Green Bastards, started drinking Southern Comfort with lemonade. It was incredibly sweet and he wasn't sure he liked it, but he liked the advert for it that they showed every time they went to film club and he thought it might be kind of cool. He threw up, very stickily, in the busy Carlton toilets with the sound of Wizzard and Slades's festive singles ringing in his ears.

Julie rubbed his back for him as they stood at the outer edge of the vast, dark ballroom. He had to admit that Liz had been right, and the blind girl did indeed give good post-vomiting backrubs. 'You mustn't think this is why we ask you along on our nights out,' he told her, and his voice sounded blurred to him under the terrific noise and the pounding in his head.

'Hahaha!' Julie went. 'You piss-head!'

She was chiming in again, but David felt cross. He felt like telling her, he hardly ever got drunk. In fact, this was the first time in his life he'd ever really drank to excess.

'Three whole weeks away from each other!' Julie said. 'Our little gang is splitting up.'

He nodded and smiled. 'Yeah, I guess so.'

'You will come and visit me in Manchester though, won't you?' she said.

He agreed, though the idea travelling anywhere made him feel like he was about to throw up again.

'Mind, you can't get in a state like this when you visit us,' Julie warned him. 'Mummy will wonder who on Earth I'm making friends with!'

Soon it was time to find Liz – she was in the Chill-Out Zone, snogging someone lanky from Business Studies they'd never seen before. They had to run to get the last free bus and they found that the top deck was, as promised, a pretty vile place to sit for the hour it took them to get back to campus.

They wandered back messily up the central walkway to Liz and David's college and Liz got them singing Christmas songs again. David hadn't realised he knew so many.

They noticed that the boards had been stripped of posters and flyers and painted over black. For three weeks campus was going to look briefly respectable and tidy again.

The three sat up in their top floor kitchen drinking cup-a-soups and eating the last of the biscuits. There was a bit of a tussle over deciding whose floor Julie was going to sleep on. They decided that they couldn't send her tap-tapping all the way down the length of campus at three in the morning. Anyhow, she'd lost her white stick at some point during the hokey-kokey. In the end she wound up in the chair in Liz's bedroom, using towels and Liz's cardy for blankets. It turned out she snored really loudly and oddly.

And then, because they were late getting up and they all felt so parched and unwell and very un-Christmassy indeed, their farewells were a rushed affair down in the porter's lodge. David emptied his room (there was a conference on and the college needed to use every inch of space) and he dragged his three bags on the bus into town, where he waited patiently for the bright blue coach to arrive to take him home, back to the bosom of his family in County Durham, in time for Christmas.

*

Two Months Later

'Oh God, she's going to mind, isn't she?' David said glumly.

He was staring at windswept fields and February rain coming down in sheets. Their train was ten minutes from Manchester Victoria and, just when he should be excited, he was feeling guilt-racked.

'Yeah, well, she's busy, isn't she?' Liz shrugged and returned to her magazine. She was alternating between Hello! and a hefty library volume about the Theatre of Cruelty. 'Doesn't she have some kind of test for her tap-dancing class today?'

He nodded. 'But we could at least have asked her. It's her city, after all.' Now he was feeling terrible. Plus, he hadn't brought a brolly with him. Still, in his head there was something terrifically romantic about the thought of Manchester in the drizzle. It made him think of Morrissey and 'William, it was Really Nothing.' Songs like that. He had on his denim jacket and his new, ever so slightly flared jeans, plus patent leather Doc Martens Liz had helped him choose. He was feeling quite excited about their day out, all told. 'Fancy having a test in tap-dancing,' he said.

'Julie reckons that even though it's an extra mural class she can still get credit if she does well.'

David was amazed. 'Credit in an English degree for tap-dancing!'

Liz nodded over her mag, reached across and opened another bag of crisps. 'She told me it had something to do with meter and rhythm, like poetry, you know? But maybe she was just having me on...'

David thought she probably was. Sometimes they underestimated Julie's sarcasm. It was as if no one expected the blind to be ironic. 'I still feel bad, though,' he said, as the train swished past ancient warehouses and abandoned factories. Liz frowned at him, so he kept his thoughts to himself as they slid under the high ceilings of Victoria.

It was just a little day out. No big deal. Just a chance to spend some time together and run around being daft. No reflection on Julie. She'd want to go and do something cultural, when all Liz really wanted to do was visit the secondhand clothes emporia in Afflecks Palace, and the record shops of Oldham Street.

David was content to be dragged along in her wake, enjoying the noise and the bustle of it all. He laughed as Liz zipped in and out of cubicles, trying on harem pants and choosing a pair decorated with marijuana leaves. She also bought herself a hat with a huge floppy brim, which she insisted on wearing for the rest of the day. Not wanting to be left out, David found himself a green velvet smoking jacket for a fiver at a bazaar and put it on at once over his denim, with both collars pulled up just so.

Both he and Liz thought they were absolutely *it* that afternoon.

They bought Thunderbird spiced wine and sat in a small park near Granada studios, sipping it straight from the neck of the bottle, feeling like the chicest vagrants in town. Liz was watching the fellas going by. 'I love all the men in Manchester. They're so beautiful with that very dark hair and pale skin. It must be the Irish in them, don't you reckon?'

He nodded dumbly. And then they were off, for another round of shops and Liz pointing out the sights to him. She came from Blackpool, which wasn't all that far. But when she'd been smaller, this had been the big city to come to, for shopping and drinking in the sophisticated ambience. 'Don't you feel like you're right in the middle of the world?' she asked him as they walked by the canal, where they were just starting to gut the old warehouses and put up new buildings. 'This was all, like, the Industrial Revolution and that. It started right here, where we're standing.'

He'd read about some of this. He'd read Elizabeth Gaskell and a bit of Engels and all that stuff. He remembered watching 'A Taste of Honey' on the telly with his mam, several times. It was her favourite film because it was about a young girl having a baby out of wedlock and having to scrape by alone. It had been filmed all round here, by the murky canals and sooty buildings and bridges. It all looked like L S Lowry in the film, and it did so now, even in 1989. 'I dreamed about you last night,' he said, quoting from the film. 'And I fell out of bed twice.'

'Did you now?' Liz smirked, and linked arms with him again, tossing the bottle into the nearest bin and clamping her ridiculous hat down on her head. 'I feel a bit pissed now. What time is it?'

It was time to start heading back to Victoria, if they were wanting to get back at a decent hour. They dashed down Deansgate, feeling a lot less chilly and damp, even though it was tipping down by now. They raced up the canyon of teatime traffic and David kept tight hold of Liz's hand as she showed the way. It struck him that, if they got separated, he wouldn't have a clue where he was. They'd roved through the city's intricate streets so thoroughly that he was completely lost by the time night began to fall.

But they made their train just in time, stopping only to buy a large bag of Monster Munch crisps and some cans of lager.

All the way back they kept up a long, complicated conversation that involved them telling each other more about their families. Some of this stuff they'd both already heard, but the dampness and cold, and the tang of the alcohol gave their stories a greater urgency and pathos. Also, they were conscious that there was a bloke sitting opposite hanging on their every word, so they were both showing off slightly, and exaggerating the tales they were spinning. Just as Liz was into her stride, describing her hippyish and slightly crazy divorced parents, the lad opposite leaned across and asked if he could share a tinny and a ciggy with them.

'Of course!' Liz encouraged him and waved him over to sit at their table. She'd been giving him the eye since Preston, and he'd been doing the same. A leggy, tousled brute with a skinny chest and a Mr Whippy complexion. She offered him a Silk Cut.

'Do you know they put little holes all around the filters in Silk Cut, so you never get a good puff on one?' he asked. He looked slightly stoned to David, who he was sitting right next to by now. Also, David was feeling that this Gothy bloke was encroaching on their day out. Their tiny gang of two was compromised by his sprawling presence. His skinny leg was squashing carelessly against David's and it was disturbing him.

Liz kept him chatting. She drew him in with that magnificent smile of hers. She glimmered at him from under her shapeless hat, which she still hadn't taken off. At one point she did a catwalk demonstration up and down the aisle of the carriage to show off her marijuana trousers and the Goth bloke clapped and jeered.

'Tell you what,' he told Liz, just as they were almost home. 'I really fancy you.'

'Ah, cheers, love,' she said, and patted his hand across the table. She never had any problem accepting compliments, David thought woozily. It was quite a skill. Mind you, he thought: she was bloody awful at taking any kind of criticism, so maybe these things balanced out.

Then he heard the Goth bloke saying: 'Tell you what, I fancy your friend here, too.'

David felt a prickle of embarrassment creep over him as he turned slightly and saw that the fella was looking straight at him. Pale and serious, and a bit sexy. Suddenly David found he couldn't breathe.

'Our stop, chuck.' Liz gathered all her stuff into her oversized beach bag and grasped David's arm as the train pulled to a stop. She looked at the stranger as he got up to let them slide out. 'Are you getting off as well?'

He sighed and sat back down. 'I wish,' he shrugged.

*

On the bus to campus, Liz and David took their usual seat right at the front of the top deck. She was moaning about losing out on the Goth fella. How fanciable he was. How they should have persuaded him to get off the train early. 'What's the big deal about Kendal?'

'Maybe it's where he lives?' David was in abstracted mood, staring at the pale towers and steeples of campus as the bus wound its way up the hill.

'Yeah, well he could have taken a detour,' Liz said. 'Taken a chance and had an adventure. That's what it's all about, isn't it? Sometimes you don't have to just go the straightest way home.' She glanced at David. 'What's got your goat, anyway? Why are you so quiet? Didn't you have a nice time today?'

Of course he'd had a nice time. He couldn't even say how nice a day it had been. There'd been nothing in particular to do. Just having fun. Making it up as they went along. Pleasing themselves. He could hardly put it into words. Whenever he went places usually, he felt the onus on him to buy presents for his mam, his sister... something small, a token thing. Something to make up for the fact that they were stuck at home, while he was out enjoying himself. But here he was, and it felt a long way from them. He was returning from a day out and it was to his new home. He felt giddy with the freedom of it all, and there was no way of explaining this to Liz without sounding a bit daft.

'That bloke,' she laughed, tutting and shaking her head. 'What was he like?'

'He was just talking rubbish.'

'No, I think he meant it. He seemed as if he really fancied us both.'

'Huh,' said David. 'What do you reckon he'd have said if I'd turned round and kissed him?'

Their bus was swerving boldly into the underpass, and others were getting up, preparing to clamber off. Liz grabbed his arm. 'What?' she gasped. 'Are you gay then?'

She was always so frank. She didn't mind asking anything. She never cared if anyone heard her. Liz's attitude was always: let them listen. I've got nothing to hide. But as they joined the small crowd swelling up the stone steps from the underpass, and up into the concrete heart of campus, David was just about hyperventilating. She was saying stuff that he hardly ever thought to himself, let alone said out loud.

'Are you, then?' she asked again, doggedly. 'It's just you've never said. And it would make a lot of sense, if you were.'

'What? How would it make sense?' He knew he had gone a funny colour. He picked up his pace, heading for the central walkway, convinced that everyone was eavesdropping. Liz came hurrying after, swishing her new trousers and clamping her hat down.

'You've never had a girlfriend in the five months I've known you. You never talk about girls in that way. Yeah, you tick all the boxes, I reckon. Come on, David. Tell me!'

He stopped and laughed. 'Stop it! Stop saying things outdoors!'

'What?' she looked mystified. 'What are you on about?'

'Just… shush!'

'What, are the Homo Police going to be after you?' She wheeled around, as if looking for them. 'They can't lock you up just for saying it out loud, you know.'

But they could. He knew they could. Every little bit of him was screaming that they could.

He led the way quickly to their college house block and she hurtled after him, determined. 'You've got to talk about this! You can't go keeping this stuff hidden away inside. Talk to me!'

He almost shouted at her. 'There's nothing to tell! I've never done anything! With anyone! Ever!'

This was right outside the porter's lodge and drew a few glances.

Liz rolled her eyes. 'You don't have to shout.'

She dogged him up four flights of stairs to the top of their house block. While he shut himself in his room she dashed to the kitchen to make a brew. Hot sweet tea, she thought. He looked like he was in shock.

Then, carrying both mugs in one hand, she knocked on his door. Gently.

When he let her in he looked a bit pale and sickly.

He'd lit a joss-stick, candles in wine bottles. He'd put his tape of 'Hunky Dory' on. 'Look, I was just saying stuff. It just came out.'

'It certainly did,' she said, sitting down on the bed with him, handing him his tea. She looked at him levelly. 'You've never told anyone this before, have you?'

His hair wanted cutting. It was hanging down over most of his face. He was really going in for that shaggy, baggy Indy look. She wasn't sure it suited him.

'David, look at me. It's not as big a deal as all that. Yeah, you've told me something you've kept secret all this time. It just came out.'

'I shouldn't have said anything...'

'Why? Why ever not?'

He looked at her searchingly. 'You won't tell anyone, will you? Please, Liz...'

'Of course not. I'm not a gossip.'

He nodded. It was true. She was lots of things, but she wasn't a gossip. Liz was the person that other people did their gossiping *about*.

'Look, chuck,' she said. 'If you're gay, or bisexual, or a transvestite or whatever, it doesn't matter to me. I'll be glad for you either way. It's not a great big scary thing at all, you know. It makes no odds. You've gone and made it into something huge and frightening for yourself, haven't you?'

He looked at her dumbly. He felt like she must do when she was at those sociolinguistics lectures with the young Swedish tutors. When everything they said seemed completely incomprehensible, even though they acted like it made complete sense.

'I don't know…' he said. 'I just…'

'You've not signed a contract with the devil, you know. And you haven't opened Pandora's Box. There are loads of gay people out there. Even here. Especially here.'

'But… if I did anything, or if I said anything… it would just about kill them at home. My Mam, my Nanna…' He couldn't even imagine how they'd react. He couldn't even picture sitting in the front room at home with them and saying anything as bizarre as the things he was saying today. What had happened to him? Was it the spicy Thunderbird wine and all the dashing about? It was like something inside him had fizzed up, and wouldn't go back down…

Liz snorted. 'What, if you tell them you're gay, your Mam and Nanna would just drop dead out of shock?'

'They'd be upset. They'd never want to see me again. I'd never see my little sister again…'

'Bollocks,' Liz snapped. 'I'm telling you this right now. That's absolute bollocks. That will never happen.' She put her arms on his shoulders, forcing him to look at her. She was so touchy-feely. It made him squirm. But now he looked into her face. 'You listen to me, David. It might take them a while to understand it all, or to understand you. But they love you. They know who you are. This is part of you. If you're gay then they're just gonna have to accept that. And they'll see that in the end. They have to.'

'It's not as easy as that…'

She took off her floppy hat and slung it onto his armchair. 'Yes, it is. This is your life, lovey. And I think it's about bloody time you started living it.'

*

It was a few days later, and they hadn't seen anything of Julie.

Liz was in rehearsals for a 'devised piece' in the large theatre, and staying there for long hours, sometimes through the night. David spent more time with the others in their house block gang, sitting with Kevin and Belinda in his room, having more of their 'long conversations about life, the universe and nowt,' as Kevin put it.

It was a time for books, too, as David threw himself at last into his reading lists, mindful that this was the term when all the long essays were due. The blue faux-leather novels his Mam had bought him for Christmas were all Victorian, and he wouldn't be reading those till next year. This first year was just Post-War stuff, and he was mired in nature poems about potatoes and foxes, and miserable ones about secretaries and graveyards. The novels were slightly less grim, some were even quite good. But the plays he found impossible. One Tuesday he had a seminar on Harold Pinter that was filled with so many awkward pauses that it seemed to last about seven hours.

He was trying not to talk too much in seminars, after realizing that he was sounding too keen and everyone else, slouching in their seats, was glaring at him. It happened in almost every subject. He backed off a little. The Pinter was the worst. The tutor on that course didn't seem to mind that no one was talking.

He was very fat, wearing a knitted tank top, beaming into empty space during the protracted pauses.

'Have you seen your girlfriend?' Liz asked him, that teatime in the square. They went to fetch groceries from the Spa, where the girls at the tills had broad Lancashire accents and Liz delighted in impersonating their calls to each other between the aisles: 'Mand-eh! Trace-eh! Wend-eh!'

'I saw her briefly, the other day,' he shrugged. 'I think she's got a lot going on.'

'She keeps herself busy, that one,' Liz said, filling her basket with pink wafer biscuits, chocolate fingers, Cadbury's cream eggs. 'She's always dashing about. You should do the same. Join a few societies. You're always moping about your room with your books.'

'That's what I'm supposed to be doing!' They stood by the conveyor belt, David unloading milk, instant coffee, sliced white bread and jam.

'You know what I mean,' she gave him a meaningful look. 'Like, you should join GaySoc.'

'Ssssh!' he was alarmed.

'They meet Thursday night in the Chaplaincy Centre. They make banners for marches and organize trips out to the theatre, or to Flamingo's Night Club in Blackpool. They hire a minibus and everything.'

'How come you know so much about it?'

'One of the third years. Tom, who's directing our devised piece. He's a puff as well. I've been picking his brains. We were having coffee at the bistro last night and I asked him what all the queers did round here. You don't mind me saying 'queers', do you? Tom says that's the preferred term these days.'

'It isn't my preferred term!' David said, blushing madly as Wendy scanned each item in his basket. She was busy bitching with Mandy across the way, and wasn't very interested in what Liz was saying anyway.

'I think Tom's quite radical, actually,' Liz said thoughtfully. 'He wears eye shadow and black nail polish and doesn't even try to hide the fact he's a puff. Well, why should he? And the play's going a bit gay, too, under his direction.'

David was glad to get out of the shop. Liz was going on too much, as usual. 'Here,' she said. 'Come and stand by me in the bookshop while I shove some set texts up my jumper.'

'They've put that new alarm system in.'

'I can get the tags out with my nails. Come on.'

When they got back to their kitchen on the top floor, they found that Kevin was entertaining a visitor who'd come looking for them. He flashed them a look, like he'd been lumbered with her. Julie was sitting at the table, eating a Kitkat and drinking tea. 'So there you are!' she said, swinging round sightlessly as they hefted their shopping bags into the room.

'Eh-up, Julie,' said Liz, still putting on her exaggerated Wendy accent.

'I've been hanging around here for ages,' Julie said. 'Luckily Kev's been wonderful company. He's like a proper gentleman.' Kevin looked a bit flustered. The door to his room across the corridor was open and his Tracey Chapman record – which David couldn't stand – was playing. 'He's made me about seven mugs of tea in a row, and kept me chatting away, even though he must have better things to do.'

Kevin went off, shortly after that. He had his own show on campus radio that started at seven o'clock. He was still pretty new to working the studio and all the complicated controls, so had to get there early. 'Bye, Kevin!' Julie called after him. 'We'll listen in! Play me a request! Anything by Spandau Ballet would be smashing. I love 'Through the Barricades,' I think it's so meaningful.'

Kevin beat a hasty retreat down the corridor, his trainers squeaking on the lino.

'Is he good-looking?' Julie asked them.

'He is,' said Liz. 'Very.'

'Wow,' Julie said. 'This place is like heaven. I hate my college. It's full of rich wankers.' The sudden bitterness in her tone surprised them both. It wasn't at all like her to swear. Julie was definitely in a funny mood.

They sat in David's room, as usual. He made toast and they spread it with jam and listened to Enya and then recent John Peel shows he'd taped off the radio. He was listening to more shoe-gazing Indy guitar bands than ever.

'I hate it,' Liz said, 'but at least it's modern. When you first came here, everything you listened to was ancient. Bowie and Lou Reed and stuff.' In front of a whole roomful she had once derided his 'Don't Walk, Boogie' tape. It was a vinyl album from K-Tel that he'd loved since he was a kid. It made him think of rainy nights on Broadway in the New York he pictured inside his head, and thumping noise from night clubs up dark alleyways and fire escapes and glitzy worlds hidden deep within the city's heart.

But Liz took the cassette out of the machine, saying it was cheesy and old-fashioned and didn't he have anything by the Bangles? 'Eternal Flame' was one of the songs of that term. Wherever you went on campus, someone was playing it and somehow it chimed with David's feelings of aching loneliness and acute longing for something he couldn't even quite picture…

It was much later, and David was explaining to Liz all about 'The Beast from the Stars.' She had noticed the fraying paperback on his bedside table, which he was reading for the umpteenth time.

'But it's a kids' book, right?'

'Sort of. But it's… like, everything. It's about everything. It's the biggest, grandest, most wonderful book I've ever read.'

She reached for it, and he winced, as if she was going to spoil it. 'I'll have to give it a whizz sometime. I'm not a big reader, though, as you know. When I saw the lists of everything they expected us to read on the courses and stuff here, I nearly shat me pants.'

Julie muttered, 'At least you don't have to have them in Braille, or have them read to you.'

'Huh! I'd love it if someone came round and read them to me,' Liz grinned. 'Preferably some gorgeous bloke. And he would read a couple of pages and then he'd notice me, sort of lying there, in my nightie on the bed, with the shoulder straps down and I'd be like, 'Oh, could you come and sit a bit closer, chuck? Whisper that into my ear…''

Julie tutted at her. David was surprised. She had a right face on tonight and didn't seem to mind who knew it. There was tension in the air, and he could sense that Liz was getting irked, too. Forever the peacemaker, David launched into an excitable monologue about 'The Beast from the Stars' and how the TV show had been the way he'd got into it, and how, even though it was just a one-off with no sequel, there was still a legion of fans out there. Last time he'd been to his favourite Sci-fi and comics shop in Newcastle, he'd even picked up a fanzine all about it.

'Well, I'd never heard of it,' Liz said. 'Have you, Julie?'

'Yeah, it's one of my favourite books too, actually,' Julie said, slightly snappishly.

'Oh, is it?' said Liz, copying her tone. She gave her a hard stare. 'Look, have you got a problem with me tonight, lady?'

The question stayed in the air for a horrible, stretched-out moment. It was worse than the Pinter seminar. His cassette recorder went thunk and David hurriedly dug out his tape of the 'Beast from the Stars' soundtrack album. It was all electronic wibbles and whooshes by the BBC Radiophonic Workshop, but was actually quite calming.

'I don't have a problem, no,' Julie said.

'Well, you've been going on weird,' Liz told her. 'You ought to stop being so frigging moody.'

*

It all came out at midnight, when they took a walk across campus, over the fields and along the motorway going south. It was something they did a few times that spring, when the nights became shorter and the skies over the distant bay and the nuclear power station were so wide and clear and huge. David's bedroom suddenly felt too warm and smoky, and it was time to put on cardies and scarves and take a walk along the edge of the concrete ghost town, and then beside the hedgerows and under the sodium lights of the M6.

Julie came with them, though her mood had darkened even more as the night went on.

They headed for their usual destination. About two miles down the motorway there was a 1960s style services with a flying-saucer shaped restaurant suspended above six lanes of traffic. It was open all night and its tall yellow windows gleamed spectrally over the dark countryside. They served perfect, golden-brown chips from their deep fat fryer and their tea was stewed dark and sweet. David and his girlfriends had made it a tradition this term that they'd come here when there were only a few sleepy souls around and have hot, salty chips after midnight.

But even the best chips in the world wouldn't mollify Julie tonight.

She hardly touched her bowl. Then, at last, she asked: 'What's going on with you two?'

'Hmf?' said Liz, who was eating like she hadn't all day. ('I've the metabolism of... I don't know, some very tiny, really busy woodland creature. That's what Tom – my director – says.')

'You two,' said Julie. 'You're up to something. Or there's something going on. That I don't know about.'

'There's nowt, honestly,' said David. He felt a jab of fear. Julie had obviously intuited something profound. That strange blind-person's sixth sense was alerting her to David's deepest secrets, which he was still uncomfortable about having aired.

'You had that day out,' Julie said.

'You what?' Liz narrowed her eyes. If there was one thing she couldn't stand, it was other people feeling sorry for themselves without due cause.

'You had a lovely day out together. In Manchester. And I'd said! I promised! I was going to show you both all around my city... I'd have loved to have gone with you...'

'You were frigging tap dancing,' Liz snapped. 'Plus, lady, I know my way about Manchester pretty well myself, you know. I don't need...'

'*What?*' Julie shouted. 'Some blind girl? You don't need some blind girl showing you around?'

A couple of lorry drivers with messy hair looked up from their plates of sausages, alarmed by Julie's yelling.

'Shurrup, Julie, man,' David said. 'People will think we're arguing.'

'I felt so left out,' Julie wailed. 'It's been like this all my life. I was never anyone's proper friend. I was always on the edges. I was so easy to leave out.'

'No wonder!' Liz shouted at her, pushing her empty bowl away. 'Are you eating your chips or what?'

'Have them!' Julie screamed, and stood up quickly. 'You can stuff them up your big fat bumhole.'

'Julie, where are you going?' David watched her tottering off to the escalator with her replacement stick swishing about.

'Just leave the dozy mare,' Liz said.

'I heard that,' Julie swung round. 'You think you're so great, don't you?'

Liz smiled. 'As a matter of fact, I *do*. I think I'm pretty fantastic, actually.'

Suddenly Julie's face was red and swollen. Tears were coming down. She was wailing so that everyone in the flying saucer – even the women serving the chips and stuff – could hear what was going on. 'You just make me feel like I should be grateful all the time,' Julie sobbed. 'Like I should be grateful you're both friends with me.'

'You should!' Liz shouted right back at her. 'That's exactly right, you boring cow! You should be fucking glad!'

Then Julie was bustling away, arms outstretched, feeling for the rubber banisters of the escalator, hoping to make a swift getaway.

David glared at Liz, who was starting on Julie's chips, and then he hurried after the blind girl.

'For God's sake, Julie, you'll have an accident…'

'I don't care,' she howled, gliding quickly downwards and waving her stick. 'I *hate* her! I hate you both!'

'No, you don't!'

'I do! You're horrible to me! You're the only friends I've made here in this awful place and you both go off and do things behind my back.' She was looking over her shoulder to yell at him, and facing the wrong way. He stood gliding four steps behind her, feeling ashamed as he attracted the stares of diners coming up the other side.

'Julie, just stop…!'

But she was on the ground floor and, with barely a hitch in her pace, dashed for the automatic doors and the balmy evening air.

'Julie!'

She'd worked herself up into a right old state.

He ran after her across the forecourt of an all-night garage and it was him, rather than her, who bumped into the petrol pump. All of a sudden he was scared of the thought of her dashing out into the traffic. He held his breath in dismay as she hurtled headfirst through some ragged bushes and down a grassy embankment.

'Where's the fucking road?' she was shouting out loud. 'Where's the fucking way back home?'

Christ, he thought, as he realized she was heading straight for the motorway.

'Julie..!'

He only just caught up with her before she managed to dash out into the northbound lane.

'What the hell are you doing?' He grabbed hold of her with both arms and held her tight at the side of the road. It was a bear hug, but it was like she was the bear. A broad-shouldered, snuffling, dark little creature, hanging onto him and digging in her claw-like fingers. She buried her head in his open shirt-neck and wailed.

'I want to go home! I'm sick of it here!'

'No, you aren't,' he tried to sound consoling, even over the blaring traffic noise. They stood there clinging on, under the strobing headlights. 'You'll be okay. You've done really well. And you're fitting in fine. We're not trying to leave you out, honestly, Julie. We love you!'

'What?' She raised her face, blinking under the pinkish light. She was looking weirdly newborn and vulnerable as her anxious eyes roved all over the place. 'Do you mean that?'

'Of course! You're our mate… Just… just don't go running off into the blummin' traffic though, eh?'

'She… Liz said I should be grateful. I should be thankful that you're even friends with me…'

'Liz talks out of her arse sometimes. You know that. Come on. It'll be fine. We're gonna look for a house together, aren't we? We're all going to live in a house in town and it'll all be fab. You'll see.'

'And you won't leave me out of things?' she asked. The anxiety was so plain in her face. She couldn't see other people's expressions, he realized. She didn't know anything about how to keep her feelings from showing up. His heart went out to her then, as he understood this.

'We won't leave you out, ever again, Julie,' he told her. 'We're in the same gang, aren't we? This is us forever now.'

The Girl in the Pink Coat

Next week brings December and a new Doctor Who book from the BBC that I've got a story in. I was thinking about it being twenty-one years of doing these Doctor Who things – with lots of ups and downs and many memorable moments – some of them great, some of them dreadful...! When you write tie-in fiction you're in a curious position – both on the fringes *and* in the very heart of the story. Many of the moments I laugh about and remember are to do with turning up at public events and *not* being someone off the telly...

The most touching moment, though, and the most important for me, was the Saturday in 2007 that Cardiff's fancy new Waterstones store opened its doors for the first time and we did a signing. I was there with the two Marks (Morris and Michalowski) because we all had books out at the same time. The TARDIS was there, as well as people dressed as Cybermen, and two publicists from BBC Books. There might have even been Daleks.

The shop was busy, the queues were busy and people were swarming up the escalators to come and see the people from Doctor Who. We were wearing those grins that you do when you're somewhere on behalf of somebody else, and fully prepared to be slightly disappointing... You're not in attendance as yourself, exactly, but you're preparing to do your very best.

Halfway through our event there was an old granddad – a very shabby, skinny old man – turning up with his granddaughter. She was about seven, in a pink, ragged anorak. The sleeves were filthy and hanging in tatters. The two of them really stood out in that well-dressed crowd and that opulent new shop. The publicist nudged me and pointed them out. The girl was clutching an extremely worn copy of a Doctor Who novel – Jac Rayner's 'The Stone Rose.' It was more like a bundle of worn, mucky paper, all balled up, that she was bringing to our table.

The shop staff and our helpers were clearly keen for people to be buying new books today, but the girl in the pink coat took her place in the queue and doggedly waited, hugging her favourite book to her. When it was her turn Grandad mumbled something about it being the only book she ever looked at. I thought it was probably the only book she owned.

She pushed it carefully onto the table in front of us three writers. Amongst our water bottles, pens, Dr Who memorabilia and shiny new books. She looked at us expectantly and someone – I think one of our publicists – tried to explain to her that this one wasn't a book written by anyone here at the shop today. Wouldn't she prefer to get a brand new one signed?

The girl blinked and stared at us. What did she care about any of these new books? How was she going to understand what the woman was saying to her? She had her Doctor Who book already. She already had the book she loved.

I took it and signed it for her, and passed it to the others to sign as well. I tried to chat with her and grin, and she just stared at me, and watched her book carefully, holding her breath until it was safely back in her grasp.

The old grandad was talking to her, standing at her back. He was very gruff and talking quite roughly, shoving her forward, telling her not to be shy, and not to be holding the queue up. She wasn't quite on the point of tears, but her eyes were huge, staring at us. Then all of a sudden they were both gone, disappearing into the pushy crowd of shoppers and Cybermen. A Waterstones person said something about 'Getting all sorts coming in here today,' and about 'Folk bussing in from the Sticks.'

And that was my moment. After all the fighting and vying for work, the commissions and the continuity and the brain-squishing effort and the imagination and the infighting and the bullying and drafting and editing and chasing and ambition and joyfulness and laughter and togetherness and friends and enemies and monsters… and the feeling of not really being part of it… and then the feeling of suddenly being *right in the middle* of it… After all that experience of whirling about in the Vortex of Doctor Who… that is still my most vivid moment of all.

Saying to that little girl in the mucky pink anorak: 'Of course we'll all sign your book. It's all of ours and belongs to all of us. We all write the same stuff together and we're glad you've brought your copy today. It's the most wonderful storybook in the world, and it'll be our honour to sign it for you.'

The Wizard of Arncliffe Place

'Hello, there!'

There was an old man standing at our garden gate. He had a great long beard, a bit yellow at the end, and an anorak buttoned all the way to the top, even though it was a warm day in spring. On his head he was wearing a huge floppy hat with a brim that put most of his face in shade. What we could see of his face looked friendly enough.

I looked at Mam, who was sitting outside our kitchen door on one of our dining room chairs. She was knitting and looked up, surprised to hear a strange voice.

'Hello again!' said the old man.

I was sitting in the dog's kennel. I liked the smell. I know that sounds weird, probably, but I did. I missed our dog, Chip, and I liked to sit there reading. I was small enough to get right in there. On hot, bright days like that one enough light came through the gaps and knots in the wood to read by. I was in the middle of a very exciting novelisation of a recent space movie I hadn't been to the pictures to see.

The old man tried again. How had he opened the gate without either of us hearing it? The gate was on the latch, because of when we used to have Chip. Now the old man was standing there and waving his arms at us. He had a long, knobbly walking stick in one hand. 'Helloooooooo!'

Mam was just staring at him, and so was I. Then we remembered our manners. 'Erm, hello?' Mam said, standing up.

She was looking very pretty that day. She had on her new, bright white jeans that she had bought at the market. And that green top, with the slightly fluffy material. It was the exact green of the shampoo we used. Her hair was long, dark and shining and I thought: Yes, that's my mam. To a stranger like this old man, she must look very pretty and young, and I was proud of her.

'I'm a bit thirsty,' he said, with a small cough.

'Oh!' said Mam. Actually, he did look very parched indeed. He was leaning on our fence now and it was as if he was about to faint.

Mam told me to fetch him a glass of lemonade (the Pop Man had been round that afternoon and we had a selection of three different kinds!)

'Just a glass of water would do,' said the old man in the pointed hat. 'I'm a silly fool. I've walked all the way from the Yellow Houses to come here and there's no one in.'

By the time I'd been indoors and filled a tall glass from the tap ('Council Pop' Mam always called tap water) Mam and the old man were deep in conversation. I'd missed some, but from what I could make out, he was the father of our new neighbour, Andrea, and it was she and her family who were out this afternoon.

'They went off to the fair,' Mam explained, as I lifted the water glass as high as I could.

'Thank you, young man,' he smiled, and didn't seem at all surprised by my smallness. Usually people have something to say about it, but this old gent just took out a very large, crumpled handkerchief from his anorak pocket and mopped his brow.

There was a strange smell. Not a horrible one. But definitely a strange one. Spices, maybe. He smelled a bit like the hippy shop in town, where they had incense and stuff burning.

'I would have phoned ahead, usually,' he sighed. 'But they're not on the phone yet. Or I might have sent a message with a blackbird. They're quite reliable.'

Mam looked at him as if she didn't know whether she was supposed to laugh or not. She smiled at him instead, and introduced us. 'I'm Helen. And this is my son, Kevin.'

The old man stared at us, one at a time, as if he was memorizing the pair of us. 'Yes, yes, I've noticed you both before. I thought you two seemed like a very nice family, actually. And living right next door to my daughter and her rabble. I did worry that you'd had a lot of noise and fuss to put up with these past few weeks…'

'Oh, not at all,' said Mam. 'It's been very quiet.'

She wasn't telling the truth. Since our new neighbours had moved into Phoenix Court there'd been an awful lot of noise. Especially in the evenings. Mam had even said she thought they might be a 'bit rough.'

The old man was chuckling, as if she knew she wasn't quite telling the truth. He extended a handful of long, crinkly fingers and she reached up to shake it. 'I'm Arnold,' he said. 'Arnold Tweet.'

Mam gave him one of her brightest smiles.

Actually, she said to me later that night, she had seen him before. She had glimpsed the nice Mr Tweet going in and out of next door several times since his daughter and her family had moved in. He seemed like a proper, old-fashioned gentleman, and it was no surprise to her that he had introduced himself so formally to us.

'It's nice that he did that,' Mam said, as she washed up our hot chocolate mugs, last thing that night. We'd just finished watching our serial on the telly. 'Most people round here don't talk to each other. They don't think to tell you who they are, or ask after you. They just get on with their own selfish stuff. You could be lying dead in your own front room and it would be years before anyone even knew...'

Mam's imagination often took a gloomy turn late at night. Especially after we had been watching our murder serials together. Really, they were too grown-up and scary for me, but she liked having the company when she watched them.

Mam loved to watch murder serials because, she said, they allowed her to indulge in her fantasies about getting revenge on my dad and his rotten family.

Tonight though, she was less gloomy than she often was late at night.

It had been a warm, beautifully sunny day on our Estate. Our little back garden had been like a sun trap. She had brought the kitchen radio out and it had been a lovely couple of hours in the sun before our tea.

Plus, we had met the magical Mr Tweet.

Yes, he was magical. He was a wizard. Even then, even before he had done anything at all to prove it, we both knew already that it was so. And his tiny little visit, having a glass of water at our garden gate, had somehow put us both in a good mood.

'I'll be off then,' Mr Tweet had smiled, handing back his glass. 'And I will be seeing you two again very shortly, I imagine,' he added.

Funny thing was, when he went, two black birds and a sparrow, who had been resting in the nearby skinny trees, got up and flew after him.

*

After that I paid particular attention to comings and goings next door. They were a strange bunch. Rowdy and they seemed like they wanted to keep separate from everyone else on our Estate. At least, that's how it seemed at first.

I found them all a bit frightening, because they were so large. There was a mother, a father and two sons and they were all huge. Tall, and quite fat. Also, they were grey and lumpy, with dark little eyes.

'I think they're trolls,' Mam said, when she saw me paying attention to the neighbours. 'I've seen them before. There were some who lived near us when I was a kid. Usually they live under bridges and things, away from humans. But this lot have managed to get a Council House…'

Trolls! Of course, that's why they looked like they did. That's why they grumbled and growled and loped about the place, and why they were so noisy at night. I knew all about them from books I had read. In stories trolls were terrifying things. They lay in wait under bridges and when you tried to cross over they would grab you by the ankles and try to eat you.

'Are they really made out of rock?' I asked Mam, peering through the venetian blinds in our kitchen. The troll family were coming back from the supermarket, it seemed, and they had pushed the trolley all the way home. Perhaps no one had dared tell them they were supposed to give it back?

'How can they be made out of rock?' Mam said, busy with turning fish fingers in the grill pan. 'How can rock be alive?'

I didn't know, but that's how they looked to me. They looked like everything I had read about them.

They were having some difficulty pushing their stolen shopping trolley through their garden gate. It wasn't the kind of thing Council planners expected anyone to push into their garden. Their shopping was piled so high items were sliding off and falling onto the ground. They had bought pillow-sized multi-packs of savoury snacks and crisps; huge tubs and boxes of sweets; jumbo boxes of sickly-sweet cereal. Yes: that was another thing I remembered. Trolls loved anything sweet. They could never get enough sugar.

All of them had long, greasy, dark hair and none of them looked anything like the nice old wizard who'd stood by our gate the previous night. Not even Andrea, who was supposed to be his daughter.

Andrea was the most fearsome-looking one of all. She had fangs like a hippopotamus and a bottom to match.

'Stop spying on the neighbours,' Mam scolded. She knew it was a bad habit of mine. I loved to see what people were up to and I could watch for hours. It was to do with being so small, I thought. It was easy to hide myself away in good vantage points and no one ever noticed me.

Except now. Just then. Right as I was thinking this. One of the troll children – the oldest one. He turned around and saw me watching through the gap in the blinds. He glared at me and his eyes burned red into mine. I jumped backwards.

'Stop messing with the blinds, Kevin. Look – fish finger sandwiches! Do you want to put on your own ketchup?'

*

It had been just my Mam and me for about three months. We liked it. When Dad was still here there were lots of fights between them. They had stopped seeing eye to eye long ago, Mam said.

Dad used to put me to bed and tell me fairy tales. That's what he was supposed to be telling me, but mostly he told me about him and Mam, and how it had been when they first got together. How everything was great. But they were both kids back then. Soon enough, he told me, responsibilities start coming in and things get tougher.

I used to wish he'd go back to telling fairy tales. I hinted at this and he had a go at making up stories again, but they all came out sounding just like real life.

*

After that we saw the old man more regularly. He made it part of his routine, when he came to visit our new neighbours, to stop by and wave hello. Mam made a mug of tea for him and he drank it standing by the garden gate, declaring it to be the most delicious cup of tea he had very tasted.

'I don't know,' Mam would say. 'He's always so friendly and smiling, but I get the sense that there's something very sad about him.'

Every night the noise would get worse from the house next door. It sounded like the old man's daughter Andrea and her husband were fighting and throwing things about. Really heavy things that would crash into the walls. It went on into the early hours. Mam said, 'I'll have to say something. It's keeping you awake at night, isn't it? On school nights, too.'

At school I saw the two boys – and they stood out a mile. They were taller and had large, bulbous heads. Their skins were grey and they slouched about the place looking grumpy. Already the other kids were calling them trolls and throwing stones at them when it was home time and everyone walked home over the Burn to our estate. But the two boys didn't complain or fight back. They just stuck together, with their heads down, and walked along, occasionally muttering something to each other.

Until one day, when it all got too much. The youngest brother – Daniel – decided one dinner hour at school that enough was enough. There was a gang of boys from his class taunting him in the school yard

They were laughing about his too-large head and the way his arms were so long and his skin so scaly. His older brother had been kept inside for some reason – and there was no one there to calm him down.

He turned on them. That whole gang of boys was horrified when he turned round and let fly with his temper. Pretty soon they were screaming at the way he lashed out with his big hands, punching and slapping at them. And he wouldn't stop. He went kind of crazy. The dinner nannies came running up at the first hint of trouble – but they could hardly stop him. It took three of those big women to hold the kid back. They dragged him inside and Dan was kicking and spitting. They took him indoors to the headmaster.

It was the talk of school for several days. How they were thinking of expelling one of the new, rough boys. Andrea and her husband were called to school. Our classroom looked out on the school drive and we were doing our project on wildlife that day. I was standing on a chair, pinning drawings onto a frieze and I saw them walking up the school drive.

And they did look strange. The clothes they wore looked ragged and old. They were blinking in the bright sunlight and they trampled over the colourful flower beds.

I told Mam all about it that night. We were having pies from the bakery and mashed potato and peas and we had the local radio on, to block out the noise from next door. It sounded like they were shouting and hitting their kids. The kids were shouting back.

Mam said, 'It must be hard for them to fit in. It's always hard for anyone.'

The next time the old man came by he looked tired and sad. Mam asked him if he'd like to come and sit indoors because it was so hot that day. He could come and sit in the shade, at our breakfast bar and have a cuppa. She thought, well, I know him now. He isn't going to attack me or be funny or anything.

I was at school and she told me later how the old man had looked so grateful. He sat indoors on one of our chrome stools and drank his tea, all the while telling her a little about his family and their troubles.

Mam and I were watching our favourite soap, then sitcom, then serial and she filled in little bits that he'd told her... how they had travelled from such a distant country, and how they had only just managed to get out unscathed. Over there, they had been quite rich, compared with what they had here. They had had a big house, and a pool and even seven cars. Their house stood by itself, and it had every luxury. But they had left everything behind very quickly and had to sell for a fraction of what it was worth...

Coming here, they had had to split up. They had appealed to the council, who gave them two council houses. Andrea and her family next to us, and the old man and his wife in a house on the next estate, the Yellow Houses.

'It took them almost a year to travel right around the world,' Mam said. 'They had a terrible time. All kinds of adventures and stuff. Very dangerous. They're all lucky to be alive.'

I was impressed – both by the idea of adventures, and by how much my mam had been told by the old man.

'Is he really a wizard?'

'Of course not,' she said. 'He's just a bit eccentric and dresses up like one.'

'But they're really trolls next door, aren't they?'

'Kevin!' she scolded me. 'That's an awful thing to say. Don't judge people by their looks!'

Mam was always judging people by their looks! I didn't point that out to her though.

As the days passed I was aware of more trouble at school for the two boys, Horace and Dan. They did weird stuff. They couldn't even talk English properly. They were stupid, and couldn't read or write. They kept getting dragged in front of the headmaster, Mr Timmins, who was (according to our teacher, Mrs Peel) completely exasperated by the newcomers, the poor man. Those boys were causing an uproar: storming out of their classrooms, smashing up their desks and throwing things about.

Their teacher was Mr Kinnoul and he was tearing his hair out at them.

Then it was getting towards the end of term and it was almost the summer holidays. I thought about long lazy days on our estate and down the burn. The council were building a boating lake on our Estate. The town play scheme would be on again. There'd be long days to read in, to run about in. We weren't planning on a holiday this year – no way could Mam afford it. But the days would be fantastic round ours anyway.

And it was as summer came that I started to become friends with the troll boys who lived next door.

*

It all started because of telly in the mornings. I don't know who saw it first, but it turned out that there were all these kids' programmes on in the morning, and the boys next door had a telly in their bedroom. That seemed an amazing, magical thing to me.

Their telly was huge, and all wooden round the sides. The screen was thick glass and rounded, like an extra thick pair of spectacles. When they switched it on there was a buzz and a hiss and a crackle deep inside, like the old glass valves were thinking about it. Then, with a smell of burning dust, the picture would come to life and fill the huge screen.

Every morning that summer I sat with Horace and Dan in their room and watched strange black and white cartoons with tinkly piano music over the top and no talking; and episodes of a space serial, also in black and white, with outlandish heroes and villains and exciting cliff-hangers that made you want tomorrow's episode come along straight away.

It seemed like telly coming out of a different time and place. When I looked in the paper to see what channel they were tuned to, I could never find it. It was like the aerial on their roof was tuning into programmes from somewhere else entirely, and this feeling never left me.

Mam was pleased and surprised that I was getting on with the two boys. I'd never really made many friends of my age before: she always blamed my size. The truth was, though, I preferred my own company usually.

But this summer was different.

Not that Horace and Dan did much talking. They sat in two chairs looking at their telly and watched without comment. They didn't even laugh at the funny bits in the cartoons. They watched the adventure serials with stoney faces, their eyes flicking left to right as they followed the action. I'd be sitting in a smaller, wickerwork chair between them, laughing like I was daft, or gripping the edge of my seat. All they did was eat bags and crisps and packets of sweets. Their jaws were working constantly, grinding down boiled sweets and claggy chews. Their room was sickly with the smell of sugar.

I was a little bit afraid going round next door. Even as the days and weeks of that summer went by. It was always a bit dark and messy inside, with clothes heaped on furniture and crates still unloaded from when they had moved in. There was a smell, too. Like, unwashed clothes and leftover food. It wasn't a great smell. The boys' parents weren't that friendly, either, not at first. Their dad never said a word to me. He worked down at the town dump, chucking things over the high wall and then operating the heavy machinery that crunched all the junk into square chunks. Horace and Dan were amazed and enthralled by the machinery and how their dad could work it. One hot afternoon we walked all the way across town to see him at work and he was pleased to see them, and he showed off, squashing up all that junk.

The sight of all that junk at the town dump made me feel queasy. Dead washing machines and tailors' dummies and boxes and cracked lampshades: all these bits of people's lives. It would be so easy for someone of my size to be lost within those hills of junk forever, I thought.

Mornings that summer were for the telly, and the afternoons were for running about outside. Usually down the burn, sheltering from the blazing sun under that swaying canopy of trees. We plodged in the stream and made camps in the woods, and swung through the trees. Sometimes we set off on expeditions into the fields that surrounded our town and headed off into the countryside, taking a picnic of fizzy drinks and ten pence mixtures from the newsagent in town. We were quite intrepid that summer – staying out till seven o'clock each evening. Mam said she'd never known the like. Usually I was such a homebody. This wasn't like me at all, this staying out till all hours. But she was glad, she said. It was more normal that I wasn't hanging round at home all day, reading books and comics and staying close to Mam. She thought it was great that at last I had friends of my own and I was getting out…

I could also see that she was feeling a bit lonely, though.

But, as it happened, she had a regular cup of tea – at least once a week or so – with the old man in the wizard's hat when he happened by. She learned a little more about him and his family, and where they had come from. 'It sounded like they had an awful time getting out of their country,' she told me. 'It was like they escaped…'

'Which country was it?' I asked her. The boys hadn't been able to tell me. They didn't talk about anything much. Just a few words here and there. Never any actual details bout their lives, though.

Mum didn't know either. 'A very old country. I thought it was Australia, at first. They said they've been there. Also, Mexico and Hawaii. But where they started out from, I haven't been able to work it out. It's like they're all running away from something…'

I couldn't decide what their accents were. They all had a twang in their voices.

As time went on, Mam seemed to make friends with Arnold Tweet's daughter, Andrea.

It all started because Andrea came to sit on her doorstep when the sun was over our front yards in the middle of the afternoons. That was where Mam used to love to sit, too. Mam would bring out a dining chair, and the paper, and a pot of tea and her favourite mug. She'd have the local radio playing pop hits in the kitchen and she'd have a breather for half an hour.

Her breaks were interrupted by Andrea next door who chose the same bit of the day in which to sun herself. But she brought a typewriter with her, which she sat on the concrete path, and she'd chainsmoke and clatter away at the keys.

'Do you want a can of lager?' she asked Mam one day.

'No thanks! What are you writing?'

'It's the story of my life!' grinned Andrea, and Mam said later that her face lit up. She looked completely different. Usually she looked so unhappy, with everything drooping down. But when she talked about the exciting, extraordinary, bizarre autobiography she was going to write, her face beamed with pleasure and she looked almost pretty.

*

'My memoirs are gonna be spectacular! They'll knock everybody's socks off! No one will believe the things I have seen…!'

Andrea was quite boastful, I thought. Plus, she spent more time talking about what her story was going to be like, than actually writing it. That summer Mam was her chosen audience. Mam would carry her dining room chair round to next door's garden, and Andrea would make endless pots of tea and pour them into glass mugs, heaping them with sugar.

'You wouldn't believe half the stuff she's telling me,' Mam would say. 'That woman has been everywhere and done everything. The whole family – they've had proper adventures and things, all over the world…' She looked dazed, as if she couldn't quite believe everything Andrea had told her.

'Adventures?'

Mam nodded. 'It turns out that they're on the run. Mr Tweet – Andrea's dad – really *is* a wizard. The government in their country has outlawed magic, and so…'

'Wait,' I said. 'He can really do magic?'

'They all can! They're all magic!'

'What country is it? Where do they come from?'

'She hasn't told me the name. I said, is it… Australia? That's the furthest-away place I could think of, and Andrea just laughed.'

'Well, they do have a kind of Australian twang…'

'Andrea says that they lived there for a little while… it was a stop-off point on their epic journey.'

*

Andrea had a brother called Bill, and he was a troll, too. He was a little younger than his sister, and still lived at home, with Mr and Mrs Tweet on the next estate, even though he was full-grown. 'My brother still hasn't found his place in the world,' Andrea told Mam. 'There's nothing wrong with him. He's just a bit shy. You'll like him. He's nice, deep down.'

Mam wasn't ready for dating, and she said so. She could feel that Andrea was trying to fix her up. Still, she dug around in her tiny wardrobe and brought out her favourite summer dress from last year. It had little daisies printed on it. She'd planned to wear it to the neighbours' barbecue anyway, she said.

Andrea had decided that her family was going to host a proper summer party and invite everyone from their new street. It would be a great way to get to meet everyone, and to prove that the newcomers weren't completely strange and unfriendly. She consulted my mam and the kinds of things the locals might like to eat. Mam wasn't sure – what kinds of things did we eat outside? Hot dogs and hamburgers, she said. Maybe fish finger sandwiches?

At the top of the hill that rolled down to the burn, Andrea's husband dug a large fire pit. We kids gathered round to watch on a sun-baked afternoon. It looked a little like he was digging a grave. With his shirt off, and showing all the cracks in his dark, rocky skin, he looked more like a troll than ever.

Mr Tweet the sorcerer happened by. 'Very good,' he observed. 'I'm glad they're making an effort this time. It's important to get along with your neighbors.' He smiled at Mam, gratefully accepting a cup of tea. 'Luckily my daughter's got you next door. She's never had such a nice neighbour before.'

Mam had brought out her best china, I realized. She had a dainty service of cups and saucers, white with a gold trim and pictures of dark pink roses. She'd had this as long as I'd been alive.

Usually it only came out of the wall unit for birthdays and very special visits.

It was probably the wrong stuff to have out at the barbecue, but we'd never had one before, so we didn't know. Mam had volunteered to do the refreshments, since next door were putting such a lot of effort into the meat and the buns and feeding the whole street. Mam and I laid out the wallpapering table we kept in the understairs hall, and put a proper cloth on it, and laid out the tea service. We only had six cups and saucers, so we fetched out as many mugs we could borrow from everyone. Mam thought it all looked really splendid, and it did. I was put on duty, carrying the tray with clean cups and the refreshed teapot, taking it all back and forth to our kitchen. I must have put the kettle on about forty times that Saturday afternoon.

Everything was going with quite a swing, though. There was a delicious, greasy white smoke swirling around and everyone from our street was there. They were all chattering and laughing, and introducing themselves. No one seemed surprised anymore that the people at number 14 looked like trolls.

It was my fortieth trip round the houses with the tea tray that I fell and smashed the teapot and three cups and two saucers. I leaped up and almost burst into tears on the spot. They were

Mam's most treasured belongings. The only expensive things she owned.

I'd tripped on the rutted muddy track between the houses and fallen full length and all the china was in the smallest, jagged pieces. There was no way of saving them. I stood there, just dumb, watching the hot tea sink into the yellow mud.

I couldn't let her see them. Hurriedly I knelt down and put all the pieces onto the tray and hurried inside.

The music was turned up loud. Next door had their picture window open, and the Bee Gees playing loudly on their stereo system. You could hear it even in our kitchen.

I was standing there with the tray, wondering if I could put all the smashed pieces in a cupboard, or somewhere Mam wouldn't see until after the party was over. Then suddenly Mr Tweet was standing with me.

At first he looked like a piece of the shadowy air. Indoors it was all dark and cool, compared with the bright sun outside. Then he stepped out of the gloom and startled me. He was wearing his pointed hat, clutching his ancient cane. 'It looks to me like someone's cuppa has come a cropper,' he said mildly.

'Where did you come from?' I gasped.

'I was using your bathroom,' he frowned at me. 'I wouldn't use next door's. She has many charming qualites, my daughter, but she isn't very clean. Now, what's gone on here?'

I shrugged helplessly and held up the tray.

'Oh, dear. She treasures this service.'

'I know.'

'It was very kind of her to bring it out this afternoon,' he sighed. 'Possibly foolhardy, but kind.' As he spoke he brought up his cane and waved it vaguely over the tray. There was a sprinkling of fiery dust all around his fingertips that came drifting down over the broken pieces.

Magic.

The fragments glowed briefly and began to change.

Each broken bit became a mouse. A terrified, white, rose-patterned mouse. They scattered like mad and jumped off the tray at once, leaving it completely empty.

'Ah,' said Mr Tweet. 'I'm a bit rusty.'

*

For the rest of the afternoon we made do with a variety of different mugs, and I prayed Mam wouldn't notice that her tea service had vanished.

As the party went on most of the adults were drinking cans of beer or cider anyway, and all the kids wanted pop. The afternoon became louder and more raucous. The food was delicious. The records spun by: Andrea kept dashing back through her picture window to choose new ones.

Mam was standing next to Andrea's brother, Bill. He was very quiet, staying at the edges of things. He preferred to let all the others do the talking and the showing off, and so did Mam.

'Come here and meet Mrs Tweet,' Mam called me, just as dusk was starting and the trees over the Burn were melting into the darkening sky. Our barbecue had sent smoke spreading everywhere and the whole place looked mysterious. And there was Andrea and Bill's Mam, looking quite mysterious herself. She wore a dark curly wig and large brown glasses, as if she was in disguise. She was in an evening dress that went right up to her chin and she wore the highest heels I'd ever seen.

'You are helping your mother; that is good,' she said, bending down to look over her glasses, right into my eyes. Her eyes were very pale blue, and her accent was very strong. I couldn't make out what it was. Something very exotic.

'He always helps,' Mam said. 'He's a good boy, Mrs Tweet.'

'That is good,' she nodded. 'You must call me Anna.'

'We know your husband,' I said, trying to sound sociable and chatty. 'He's very nice. He's really a wizard, isn't he?'

Anna laughed. 'Yes, he is much nicer than me, and much more magical.' She produced a packet of cigarettes and a gold lighter out of nowhere. 'My magic these days is limited to parlour tricks and making cigarettes appear out of nowhere.'

Mam smiled. 'That must be a saving, though. They cost so much these days, don't they?'

Anna Tweet looked at her as if she was crazy. I was wondering how Mam knew what cigarettes cost anyway. She'd never smoked in her life. Neither had I. I'd tried one little mouthful of smoke once, on the way home from school. It was horrible, but it reminded me of my dad's parents and their house that was always filled with yellow smoke and the Saturday nights I used to spend there.

Anna was saying something else, and I had to concentrate hard to work out her accent. 'The magic becomes fainter, the further we are from home. Back home it was an incredible thing. We could do anything. Here's it's very thin, and we are almost ordinary.' She sighed, and took a long drag on her cigarette. It drooped out of her mouth.

There were fireworks, which surprised us all. Andrea's husband had fixed them up. He oohed and clapped as they soared above the treetops and the triangular rooftops of Phoenix Court. This was after dark had fallen and the fire pit had died down, basking us all in a wonderful orange light. None of the neighbours complained about the noise, because all of the neighbours were there, enjoying themselves. I met people I'd never even seen before, including Mandy, the woman at number sixteen, who lived with her teenaged son, Tom and who Mam always said looked depressed because she dyed her white hair black at the start of every month.

It was Mandy's where everyone ended up after the party fires died down and it became too chilly to stay outside. That was something about the new people in our street – they didn't like the cold. They were keen on pointing out that the place they came from was so much warmer than here. It was a much nicer place all round.

Late that night we sat in Mandy's house and they were all getting tipsy on homemade wine and singing songs from the old country. I was amazed that we were all up so late. I kept asking Mam if this was okay, if we shouldn't be getting home. I felt like we were a long way from everything we were used to, even though we were just a few doors down.

'It's fine, love,' she smiled, ruffling my hair. This was something she never usually did. 'Don't worry. We're having a nice time.'

In Mandy's crowded living room Mam sat on a settee by the door with Bill. He had his arm around her and she was throwing back her head every time she laughed, like a girl in a shampoo advert.

Then Andrea's husband and some of the other men were trying to put up a screen for a projector. They struggled for a while with the rolled up canvas, knocking things over and getting it tangled. Mandy was sorting through cans of real, actual film and getting the projector moving. When the lights went down and everyone settled to watch I thought we were going to see cartoons, or even a nature film like we had at school, but it wasn't either of those things.

These were home movies. Through the flickering scratches and bursts of light it was soon possible to make out people's faces, and to see them crowding into the picture, waving and wearing bright clothes. Mandy, looking much younger and smiling. Her son, when he was about my age, and a man I didn't recognize. Then there were members of the Tweet family, and they were all in the countryside, showing off in front of Mandy's camera.

There were cheers and laughter in Mandy's smoky living room, as different faces loomed up and disappeared.

The scenery around them was very leafy and green, with mountains and the most lavish trees. It reminded me a bit of the Lake District, where we'd had a holiday in a caravan the last summer Dad was with us. But as one film followed another, it was obvious that this wasn't the Lake District. The mountains were immense; the forests were dense and dark. And what was that...? A glimpse of something moving between the trees; an impression of a gigantic wild animal, blowing flames out of its nostrils...? The picture juddered and altered and here was a scene of dancing baby dragons, swooping in a circle of flame...

No, I must have dropped off. It was so late and the crowded room was so hot and dark. I woke after fleeting seconds and now they were watching some other kind of movie, once the home made ones ran out. They were showing such impossible things. Ships and sea monsters and salty coastal towns, where ogres and trolls and elves went passing before the camera's lens, pointing and waving and smiling. The people on the screen were pony-trekking across snowy wastes and then they were fighting some horrible kind of pointy-headed monsters with swords and daggers. Vaguely I wondered what film this was, and why I'd never heard of it before. It was all very spectacular. The effects were pretty good.

My mind must have scrambled everything up, because then I thought I saw Mr Tweet, Arnold Tweet, that nice old man who came to our fence for a regular cuppa with Mam, holding aloft his knobbly staff and shooting purple fire and smoke out of one end. He was looking more like a wizard than ever before as he fought with monsters.

Then, the next thing I know, Mam was lifting me up in her arms. I was small enough in those days – even at the age of eight – for her to gather me up and carry me like that. I was dead to the world. She was yawning, too.

Later the next day she told me how we'd left at almost two o'clock in the morning, and she'd never been out so late in years. She said that there was light and music coming from Mandy's house till almost five, when the summer daylight came creeping back over Phoenix Court. She said that they were still singing their strange songs from the old country at that time, though more gently by then, but you could hear them all the way down our street.

Understanding

One

'Watch out for people who go putting on airs,' said Mr Child. 'Beware of people going out of their way to show you how clever they are.' He looked up from the little philosophy book he said he'd found in Durham's Oxfam shop and grinned. 'Because they're full of shite, usually. Watch out for them!'

He had dragged his chair out from behind the teacher's desk – as usual – and was sitting right in front of our class with one leg crossed over the other, holding his little book up. He smiled at us in the half-light through the black venetian blinds.

What was it with that room of his always being half in darkness? It was right at the top of the glass building, and it should have been the lightest and airiest of all the classrooms. It looked out over miles of bright yellow fields. Mr Child jumped up to adjust the bent and dusty blinds once more. He didn't like the direct sunlight, he said, so down they came, lowered noisily like a broken guillotine.

'The... man who... invented the guillotine was actually called Mr Guillotin... and he invented it especially for the French Revolution...' Mr Child was puffing and panting as he pulled the strings at his end of the blinds. I was pulling on the other end and the blinds were making an awful ratcheting noise. 'He practised decapitating sheep! On the cobbles in the street... outside his house, in a little alleyway near St Germain des Pres... in Paris. Imagine the poor sheep queueing up and watching him experimenting with his terrible machine!'

Mr Child tugged on the string and his end of the blinds shot down faster than mine. We had a lopsided triangle of shade bisecting the brilliant sunshine. 'That'll do. Will that do? Half the room's in shadow, and the rest of you can just sunbathe...' He shrugged as our class gave him an ironic burst of applause. 'What can I say? I'm a ginger fella. I can't stand being in the sun, I evaporate! Now, where was I..?'

He went back to his chair at the front and picked up his book. 'Oh, yes. Don't trust those who crack on they're intellectuals. Just watch out for them! And ornate prose styles! Oh, my god, watch out for people covering up the fact they know nothing by putting on an overly ornate prose style! That's bullshit of the highest order, that. Awful! And the worst thing is, people are taken in! If they read something they don't understand they think – ooh, it mut be clever. Too clever for me to understand!' Mr Child burst out: 'But, no! They've been hoodwinked! They've been blinded by bullshit! Absolute bullshit and bollocks!'

He flapped his book and kept shouting the words 'bullshit' and 'bollocks', and this was the bit we liked the best. He was getting excited and red in the face. He rolled up the sleeves of his grey shirt and rubbed a hand through his hair. 'Now, where was I? Aye, yes. Just think! What must have been going through the heads of those poor sheep? Besides a razor sharp blade, that is! Mr Guillotin had an arrangement with the restaurant next door and he'd pass on all the heads and bodies and grisly bits of mutton when he was finished. Forty thousand people died on the guillotine during the Revolution! Forty thousand human heads followed all those sheep! Including Monsieur Guillotin's own!'

There was a knock at the door and, without waiting, the head of German stepped into the room. 'Is everything all right in here?' Mr Robbins asked. He was a beaming, worried kind of man. He wanted the best for everyone, but something about Mr Child always made him feel nervous, you could tell.

'Aye, Mr Robbins. All fine in here. Am I being too noisy again? We were trying to fix those bloody blinds...'

Mr Robbins surveyed our class worriedly. Clearly he felt protective of his small band of A Level students. There were only three of us studying German with him and Mr Child. We were an elite band he was very fond of. He had high hopes for us. While he was our main teacher, Mr Child had the responsibility of guiding us through the Literature part of the syllabus. It was a big task. Fully half of the final exams were on books that Mr Child was teaching us. When he heard Mr Child getting excited and shouting 'bullshit!' and 'bollocks!' and playing with the blinds in the next room, Mr Robbins always became nervous. He'd come darting through to check on us all.

'We're fine, Mr Robbins,' said Mr Child. 'We're having a lovely time. Just dandy.'

'That's all right then,' said Mr Robbins. '*Entschuldigen sie.*'

'Aye, whatever,' said Mr Child and gave him a wave. The door closed again.

'Right, where was I with philosophy?' Mr Child flapped his little hardback book at us again. 'Okay, Verstand and Vernunft. That was it. Now, I've got a feeling that Emanuel Kant is the key to all of this. Verstand and Vernunft. Two different kinds of understanding. Now, does anyone want to have a go at describing the difference between the two different kinds?'

He looked up at us and his eyes were very pale and blue. He looked like he really expected us to have all the answers. He was trying not to seem impatient with us, but we really weren't on the same page.

My friend Gail asked him, 'Is this to do with Wilhelm Tell, sir? Are we still talking about Schiller?'

'Yes, yes, of course we are,' he said, impatiently, and smiled to soften his tone. 'But my feeling is that you can't read the Schiller without understanding Emanuel Kant first...'

We hadn't read the Schiller yet. We were still on the first page. After two classes on Wilhelm Tell we hadn't got very far at all.

*

We were used to going off on tangents with Mr Child. He'd get carried away. We'd encourage him. His tangents would take us further and further away from the point. They'd take up whole lessons. We loved them though.

'The moon! Lunatics! *Lunacy!* Do you know about the connections between the moon and madness? Werewolves! Legends! And... Psycho..! Who's seen Alfred Hitchcock's Psycho?' He stared at us with disbelief. 'What?! *None* of you? None of you have seen Psycho..? But it's a bloody classic movie! Where have you all been all this time..?'

'We're not as old as you,' Gail said cheekily. 'We've got catching up to do!'

'Hey, you're not that much younger,' Mr Child laughed. 'I'm only twenty-three. What's that? Five years older? When you get to my age, you'll find that's nowt. That's nowt at all! Age is an illusion! It's all bullshit! Now, where was I... Yeah! Psycho..!'

And he spent the rest of that hour acting out the whole story of Psycho. He did all the voices and actions. He crept around the classroom like it had been transformed into a chilling murder house. He mimed being Janet Leigh standing in the tub, lathering up and then shrieking when the shower curtain got ripped back. He acted out the frenzied stabbing and we sat there in amazement. Was he really going to do the whole film? He was! Right to the end.

'I wouldn't even hurt a fly...' That was the final, unnerving line and we got there eventually before the home-time bell, but not before Mr Child had taken a detour into explaining schizophrenia, transvestism and the Oedipal complex. When the bell went he grinned and took his bows and said, 'But we still didn't get to Wilhelm Tell, did we..?'

The German books we were supposed to be reading for the syllabus came out of the cupboard at the back of the room and they smelled really damp and old. The print was tiny and generations of kids from our school had written notes in pencil on every single empty bit of page.

'Verstand and Vernunft,' he kept saying, chewing on a biro. 'It's all to do with these two different ways of understanding. Can anyone help me? Does anyone know what I mean?'

And we'd struggle with the opening scenes of Wilhelm Tell again. We all knew the famous bit, with the apple on the kid's head and the arrow and all that, but we hadn't quite got to it yet. 'But it's just like last term and Brecht,' Mr Child said. 'We got there eventually, didn't we? And now you're all experts on The Life of Galileo! I could ask you anything about that play, couldn't I? You'd all know the answers in a flash. I could ask you like… like I was the Spanish Inquisition..!'

This really cracked him up. Every mention of the Spanish Inquisition during the Brecht play had made him howl. 'I know it's not funny… and they were bad buggers really, all the things they did… but I just… can't help thinking of the sketch…! You know… You know the one..?'

Then he was horrified that we had never seen the Monty Python sketch. The very next week he turned up with photostats made on the school copier. Pages from his book of Monty Python. We were all going to act out the Spanish Inquisition sketch in class and by the end we'd understand Galileo much better. And we did! We really did!

He was lugging the heavy Multimedia trolley into the classroom. He'd brought his copy of Queen's 'A Night at the Opera' on vinyl. He flapped the gatefold sleeve at us excitedly. 'Now, just listen to the words! We can sing along! *'Galileo! Galileo! Magnifico-*

oo-oo..!' He beamed. 'See? It's all about Galileo, too! Beelzebub... has a devil put aside for him! And it's the moon again, you see? The moon going round and round the world! The moon in the sky and madness! *Lunacy..!*'

So then he had the three of us taking different parts to sing 'Bohemian Rhapsody' along with the school's ancient record player.

Mr Robbins came knocking. 'Erm... that's a bit loud, Mr Child... We're doing our language lab next door...'

But Mr Child was still singing: '*Bismillah, no...!*'

Suddenly Mr Robbins was frowning. It was rare that we saw him frown. 'Mr Child,' he said, warningly. 'Turn it down. *Bitte sehr.*'

So Mr Child did.

Weeks later he harkened back to that scene and he told us: 'Now, it was my *Verstand* that gave me my immediate understanding of the situation. If I don't turn down the volume Mr Robbins is going to be very angry, and with possible awful consequences for all of us. But my *Vernunft*... that was a different kind of understanding of the situation. I *think* that's the right way round, anyway. All to do with principles and the bigger picture. Did I think it was important that I played Queen at top volume to you three, sitting here, last thing on a Tuesday afternoon? Did I think that was dead vital for your understanding of Bertolt Brecht?'

He looked faraway and thoughtful for a second. His eyes closed and you could see that his eyelashes were actually white. 'Why, yes, of course I did! *Of course* it was!' He dashed back to the blinds and started yanking on the cord again. The late afternoon had shifted and the sun was getting on his nerves. 'And do you know why? It was important because you lot – you three – because you'd remember it. And I was right, wasn't I? You do remember *all* of it, don't you..?'

Two

It's true: if I can't remember every single class we took with Mr Child, I do still remember quite a lot. Maybe that's because of all the moratoriums and stuff that came afterwards, when the three of us didn't get the grades we were supposed to, and everyone who knew us kept asking: 'But what happened? What on earth were you doing in all those German Literature classes? It was only one paper, for goodness' sake. One small part of your exam…!'

We must have failed it. Failed it utterly and completely. All three of us. That's what we realised late that summer, when the exam results came in. Or maybe we just filled every page of the essays we wrote for that exam with mystifyingly irrelevant stuff? The exam marker – paid by the hour for recognising the correct kind of things to reward – must have sat there perplexed. Fail! Fail! Useless! Irrelevant! Fail!

The printed pages with our tabulated results went up on a green felt board in the school's main entrance on a morning in August and everyone trooped in, feeling scared, bewildered and excited. Nowadays there's much more fuss, with TV camera crews taking pictures of girls jumping up and down holding bits of paper. Back in our day it was much more low key, and our Sixth Form was very small, of course. Only three of us were doing German. And all three of us barely passed it. All three of us were rewarded with D's.

'But you were all so good in your Language classes! With *me..!*' cried Mr Robbins when we saw him later that week. 'I just don't understand it. I don't understand it at all!' And that genial red face of his looked peevish all of a sudden. Someone was to blame. Someone had let down his star pupils.

I was blushing with shame. I was deciding that I would never talk German again. I would never go to Germany and I would never think about any of this again.

Here we were at the end of that week of exam results. In the noisy and boisterous Arts Centre bar in Darlington. It was a wonderful Victorian hospital where exhibitions were held, shows were put on and films were shown. The bar was always heaving and it was here that our little gang had decided to celebrate our exam success. Or commiserate, rather, because things hadn't gone according to plan.

Neither Gail nor I had made our grades. All our plans had had to change. Our first choice universities had in effect rejected us and now we stood there with our pints of lager. Bereft, ashamed and shell-shocked.

'It must have been the literature,' Mr Robbins said, several times over. 'It must have been that damned literature paper.' Then he looked at us very sorrowfully. 'What on Earth were you three and Barry Child doing all year..? I know there was lots of messing around and time-wasting, but surely... Surely you covered the syllabus..?'

Gail and I glanced at each other nervously. Now we wished we hadn't crossed the bar to go and talk to Mr Robbins on Friday night. But it was such a surprise to see one of our teachers standing at the busy bar! Smoking and drinking whisky and having friends we'd never seen him with before. They looked such a rakish and tipsy group, standing in a fug of smoke and male laughter. It had seemed important to the pair of us to go over there and... I don't know. What were we seeking? Sympathy and understanding? Someone telling us that these D-grades were a travesty? We were much better than that! Why, we talked German like natives and he was sure that an appeal would be launched against the exam board…

I think we just wanted telling that we were clever, really. Just like we'd always thought we were. We wanted to go back to before that cosy understanding had collapsed. But Mr Robbins wasn't reassuring. He went pinkish purple and looked very disappointed.

'Bloody Barry Child,' he muttered. 'Bloody hell.'

*

Several years later. I was doing a postgraduate degree at the university where I had ended up because Durham wouldn't have me with my D in German. I met a woman who'd been a teacher in a much fancier Sixth Form college than our school would ever be. Somewhere in Cheshire, she came from and she was fiercely well-informed. She was on boards and arts councils and all kinds of things. We became friends as soon as our course began. We sat in her car and cafes all over the city and trailed around bookshops and winding streets. There was always a lot to discuss.

'There's no way,' she told me firmly, appalled, when the subject of A Levels, failures, results and university places came up. 'There's absolutely no way we in our school would have let your results go unchallenged. A clever lad like you? You dropped down two grades between the Mocks and the Finals?'

'Well... there were only three of us... and there was Mr Child...' I mumbled, still vaguely ashamed about the whole German Literature affair. Even after four years. The business of Verstand and Vernunft.

My friend shook her head. 'We'd have kicked up such a stink. We'd have shot straight back to the exam board. It must have been their mistake. Two whole grades? Down from B to D? A whole cohort? No, no. It's not the students' fault. No way. That's clearly the fault of the people marking the papers and we'd tell them so.'

Then she looked at me pityingly. She winced, like she often did when she considered where I came from, and what I'd come through, to be the person I was today. This always made me feel uncomfortable. Lots of things about our friendship and its inequalities did.

'But you see,' she went on. 'This is the difference between coming from a nice school in Cheshire, where people aren't afraid to stand up for you. Where people know how to demand what they want and deserve. The difference between that - and coming from the back of beyond, where you come from.'

I always supposed she was right. It was fear and inexperience and just putting up with what you were offered. That was always the thing that would let you down.

'But it all worked out fine,' I said. 'I'm much better off where I ended up. And so was Gail, in the end. Durham was such a snobby, stiff old place. I'd never have fitted in. I think it was all serendipity in the end..!'

'Hmm,' said my friend. 'I suppose that's true enough. But still. You have to speak up for yourself. You mustn't simply accept what's on offer. And you must challenge results that you don't think are right.'

I sighed. 'They probably were right, that's the thing. We didn't prepare for the paper properly. I don't think we quite covered the syllabus…'

'Well, that's a problem,' she said snappishly. She was driving through Manchester City Centre. Fuming at male drivers.

Fuming at men generally. We'd been to a reading at Waterstones Deansgate by Jeanette Winterson and we were both furious with the patriarchy and how it evinced itself in our everyday lives. 'If you don't cover the whole syllabus, how can you expect to get anywhere? It was that stupid fucking teacher of yours. Indulging himself. Talking about just anything that took his fancy. He should have been sacked! He wouldn't have lasted five minutes in my place. I'd have torn a strip off him, the fucking fool! What did he think he was doing, messing with young people's minds like that? Messing with their future prospects! You were innocents! Typical man! Typical arrogance!'

We veered off Deansgate onto the ring road and at last we were heading out of town.

'I thought he was a great teacher,' I shrugged, looking out the window at the lights of Manchester.

'What would you know?' she laughed fondly, patting my knee.

*

I rankled a bit under that patronage, really. That friendship had been terribly exciting at first. All the books I hadn't read. The places I hadn't been. Delia had a car and she lived in deepest, darkest Lancashire, somewhere near Chorley. She bombed about in that car, all over the north. It was her freedom, after more than fifteen years teaching A level students. Suddenly she was free and studying again, for herself. Doing an MA and writing a novel. A feminist, Magical Realist novel that kept her furiously awake at night. She was finding new friends and covering hundreds of miles each week as she drove all over the north with them. Sculpture parks and theatres and obscure second hand bookshops and galleries. We were discovering all these places together because I – twenty years her junior – was her new best friend.

'To think – you'd never eaten an avocado before you met me!' she laughed. 'Twenty-two and you'd never had an avocado!'

And I'd never seen David Hockney paintings in the flesh before, either. I'd never sat in a passenger seat in a snowstorm, lost on the Pennines, careering towards what felt like our doom.

My postgraduate years were full of firsts like this. Some of them I knew I'd look back on with mixed feelings.

To me it was all learning, though. To a writer everything is material. It's all experience. And we loved each other, in that we loved each other's company. We loved making each other feel brave. Even though life was filled with unutterably boring shit – her family life, her splenetic mother who lived in their granny flat, her neglectful husband – even though all these things were pressing, when we were together it was like we lived a different life. A life in art, a life in literature. We were living the life of the mind. That's how we felt. We could be like the people in the books we loved, just by willing it so. We could be Ursula and Gudrun and Birkin in 'Women in Love.' Living our fullest, fanciest, sexiest lives. Even though anyone else might think we weren't exactly entitled to them.

 We were being writers together.

 Bits of our friendship I was never all that sure about.

 Some bits felt like we were off the syllabus.

*

I remember returning home one Christmas and telling Gail that I was having an intense friendship with a woman. An actual woman. A married woman twice my age. Maybe more than a friendship.

 'Oh, David,' she said, looking sad and stricken on my behalf. We were sitting – I can see it now! – in a café in a place called The Ginnel in Darlington. All those alternative, patchouli and herbal tea places in our old town were snuck away in mews and courtyards behind the main street. Hippy and goth shops. Vegan cake shops and second hand books and fanzines: all the stuff we loved back then. 'David... are you sure that's what you want? *Really?*'

Gail pricked my confident bubble. There I'd been at twenty-two: all pleased and proud of myself. I'd been bragging, like a fool. Like the best thing about the whole experience was telling the story afterwards.

Was that what I was after? In my paisley scarf and my hair dyed tomato soup red. Christmas in 1992. Gleaming with excitement. Like I'd graduated into being wonderfully bisexual rather than simply a straightforward puff. Like I'd evolved into something special.

Gail could see right through me, though. She'd never willingly shoot me down, but even as she told me that she was happy so long as I was happy, I knew she disapproved. I sat there miserable, with all my exciting news in tatters.

Gail smiled at me. She told me to take good care. Look after myself. Be careful.

Talk turned to Gail's drama course. She was in Liverpool. She was in a play! 'Look Back in Anger.' I promised to come and see it. 'Everything worked out for the best,' she told me, not for the first time. 'My year out. My year on the Kibbutz. Then going to Liverpool and finding my feet. None of that would have happened if we hadn't all failed German Literature.'

'Well... we didn't fail it completely...' I protested.

She laughed at this. 'Almost! But it doesn't matter. None of that matters now. Very quickly, it turned out, that really didn't matter. What matters is where you end up, and what you end up doing there...'

She was right. Gail was always right.

We went to Guru Boutique and fussed over crystals and bangles and beads. We bought cards that we knew we'd be writing and sending to each other when we returned to our separate university towns.

'I'd earmarked all kinds of fellas for you, in my year group,' Gail said with a shrug. 'And now you tell me you're straight!'

We were kissing goodbye at the end of the Ginnel. 'I'm not straight. I'm polymorphously perverse! I'm a bisexual lothario! A sexual adventurer...!'

Gail looked at me, sceptical and fond. 'Just don't get hurt.'

*

Later that day I was transported back into those summer afternoons with Barry Child. Maybe something about the sunlight filtering through dusty windows on the bus. Slantwise, like those heavy blinds in his teaching room at the top of the school. And spending time with Gail, and hearing her gentle voice. The sweetness of that spicy, hippyish perfume of hers. I was drowsy on the bus from Darlington back to Aycliffe and I could hear us all, back there in that purple classroom. I could hear us *not* doing German Literature.

'It's true! I read it in the NME! It's definitely true..!' Gail was protesting. Mr Child was in kinks of laughter. He sat forward on his teacher's chair, clutching his knees.

'It can't be true..!' he gasped.

'But it is! It is..! Leonard Cohen is recording a new album… and it's a dance record. He's recorded a disco album..!'

When Mr Child stopped laughing he started asking the rest of us whether we knew all of Leonard Cohen's records so far. We didn't? How could we not? Gail did. Gail had wonderful musical taste! Could she bring her Leonard albums in next week, and we'd all listen together? And we'd all pore over the lyrics together.

And so we did. And the following week we had a seminar on 'The Catcher in the Rye.' 'I never read this when I was your age. This is my first time!' Mr Child was very excited about Salinger. 'But you lot… you're exactly the right age, right now! Well, maybe slightly too old. Seventeen? Eighteen? But you'll get the point of it now. You'll see the wonderful point of it all…!'

We talked about Salinger for several weeks after that.

And Wilhelm Tell and Brecht and Galileo and even Emanuel Kant slipped further and further from our thoughts and understanding.

Street 1995

This was where I was more free than I've ever been.

We went to live in a tiny flat in the corner of the fourth storey of a warehouse on Thistle Street. Our windows were level with the streetlights and the only way in or out was a rickety fire escape up a narrow cobbled alleyway. At first it was dizzying, but by the end of summer 1995 we took it in our stride, running up and down those steps without even thinking about it.

My flatmate was Amanda, a friend I'd made in our university town of Lancaster. She was finishing her MA, I was writing up my PhD thesis. It got to the summer and we decided suddenly we didn't want to live as students in our northern English town any more: we wanted to live in a proper big, European city…

In that tiny flat our two closest shops were Oddbins and James Thin, where they sold every single newspaper and magazine published anywhere in the world. Our nearest café was Cyberia, where for a pound an hour you could paddle in - rather than surf - this strange new thing they called the Web.

Down on Hannover Street there were glorious smells erupting from homely Italian restaurants. We couldn't afford to eat in them, but we could sit on top of our fire escape and sniff the gorgeous reek rolling by. Same with the aroma of hops hanging over the town. The smell that defined the place. We always found money for beer, it seemed.

And we drank in the Blue Moon. The Queer café on Broughton Street, in the pink heart of the city's Gay Triangle. It was staffed by a shifting cast of glamorous Australians and open all night long. Its walls painted the darkest of blues, serving nachos and burgers and pints of fizzy lager all day and all night long.

It was the summer that Easy Listening came back. We were ironic 1990s kids and so when we went out it was to clubs playing ancient tunes on vinyl. We dressed in clothes from charity shops, denim and bright nylon, wigs and feather boas. The music was by the Tijuana Brass and the James Last Orchestra. In our twenties we recycled the trash of the past and danced in funny venues: cinema foyers and empty shopping centres.

My eyes boggled all that first summer. I was dizzy with freedom and lager and running up and down that fire escape twenty times a day...

I could afford to live because I had sold my first novel. 'Marked for Life' had been bought by Chatto and Windus for less money – my editor told me – than they'd spent on champagne at the launch of their new biography of Virginia Woolf, but it was enough to keep me going for a few months.

I was a writer in the city. I was everything I'd ever wanted to be since I'd read 'Goodbye to Berlin' when I was nineteen. I was that camera, swooping round the city and recording absolutely everything. This was the summer I really taught myself to write, I think. And I did it in the simplest way possible. I wrote about anything that came into my head, and I did it for about ten hours every day. I kept the journals I'd always wanted to keep, like proper writers did.

I took myself out into the city with a leopard print backpack and I went to café after café, bar after bar. I went with my friend Richard, who was an artist, and Amanda's boyfriend. We sat in the café of the Modern Art Gallery, of the City Café, or Iguana, or Route 66, or the Film House Bar. I would write and he would draw. He drew in oil pastel, felt tip, anything that came to hand. I wrote about the people at the next table, the conversations I overheard, I wrote about my many adventures and I wrote up all the memories I had at twenty-five.

Our tables were littered with pens and empty cups and shreds of paper. And gradually, I learned more about writing than at any other time in my life.

We'd arrived in the middle of Festival time, and so I came here to Charlotte Square. I sat in this square every day and listened to Edna O'Brien and Marina Warner. I listened to Eleanor Bron who asked her audience, 'Who here among us is secretly a writer? But you must be brave! You must put up your hand and be counted!'

It's the kind of place where you run around and get your heart broken, too. When you fling yourself headlong into life, it's bound to happen. You'll fight with your flatmate, make some dodgy friends, have some truly awful nights out. Your mid twenties can be the time when everyone goes completely bananas with their freedom. Oh, freedom to make a complete fool of yourself is such a big part of it.

My flatmate said: 'It's not the kind of time and place where you're gonna meet the love of your life. And certainly you won't, hanging out at CC Blooms every night.'

But I knew she was wrong. And, at the end of a full and complicated year, I did actually meet my beloved Jeremy at CC Blooms. We got together then and we haven't parted since. On the way up to my flat he asked my name and realized he'd bought by first novel that very same day. How serendipitous was that? He'd bought it in the bargain bin for 99p, but even so. It was in the bargain bin already? Only a year after I'd signed the contract? Only a year into my writing career and someone had put me in the bargain bin?

That's how it was in 1995. It was all pretty fast. Lots of stuff happened. Some of it came out of the bargain bin, some of it ended up there. But most of it was worth keeping for a lifetime. And I'm glad I found the space and time and freedom to write those journals.

That was the year I novelised my life.

Copyright Paul Magrs 2020

With huge thanks to Rylan for artwork and all the help! And thanks to all of Fambles – and to Jeremy, Panda and Bernard Socks.

Printed in Great Britain
by Amazon